SAFE AND SOUND

Rachel Bowdler

CONTENT WARNINGS

Death, murder, violence, blood and injury, and grief

References to alcohol and drugs

Strong language

PROLOGUE

Ruby Bright wore exhaustion like a scratchy, woollen cardigan in the middle of summer, the threads knitted into her skin and the pockets weighed down by sharp stones. She wanted nothing more than to sleep, but with her unadjusted ears still ringing in the rare bout of silence and her heart still racing in time to a phantom bass, she knew it would take hours to drift off — especially with the tour bus jolting and the engine humming beneath her as it carried her to the next nameless city, the next faceless gig.

Twelve more, she reminded herself, collapsing into the corner of the couch and burying her face into a velvet pillow. Just twelve more, and then she was back to the studio, where the chaos and the fatigue and the constant stifling pressure would ebb just enough that she could breathe again. She marked it off with a black Sharpie — the same one she'd been clutching since the end of the show, used to sign autographs and casts and sometimes bras — on her calendar, which swung like a pendulum against the bus's movements on the wall behind her. Two hundred consecutive Xs had already been penned there, spanning from March of this year until now: September.

It used to feel like an accomplishment. Now, it felt like a punishment; like she was a prisoner tallying off the end of one dragging day while already dreading the next.

"Cerys told me you haven't eaten yet." The voice came from behind her, as melodic as it was when singing beside her on stage. Ezra Lawson was its owner: Gen Y's lead guitarist, Ruby's songwriting partner (and, according to Fusion Management and the tabloids, her romantic partner, too), and her best friend. He emerged from the steps leading downstairs, where Max's faint laughter pealed in sporadic bursts. The party never ended for the bassist, nor for Spencer, the drummer, who was no doubt down there with her. For Ruby, it had ended long ago, and that was probably why the band had drifted apart of late.

"I wasn't aware Cerys was monitoring my diet now too," Ruby retorted, popping the lid back on her pen and shooting Ezra a pointed look.

With dark circles stained beneath his hazel eyes and his shirt hanging loosely off sagging shoulders, he looked as tired as she felt. His tattooed hands clutched a pizza box.

"She's monitoring everything," he huffed, collapsing onto the couch beside her and placing the box on the table. Though she was their manager, Cerys was also a dear friend and tried to help where she could; she was still a cog in Fusion's machine, and it showed in her overbearing need to

2

know what Ruby was doing, eating, and drinking twenty-four hours a day. "She's just like the rest of them, even if she doesn't know it. Her heart's in the right place though."

He opened the lid to reveal the pizza had already been half-eaten by the gannets downstairs. Ruby loved pizza, but tonight the stench of grease and fried meat left her stomach churning and she pushed it away with her slipper-clad foot. "I'm not hungry."

"Rubes." Ezra sighed and scratched his head, leaving his jet-black curls even more mussed than usual. It wasn't a scolding, though. She knew that. Only sympathy and understanding swam in his voice, and Ruby tried not to acknowledge the prickling promise of tears in her already gritty, eyeliner-ringed eyes.

"I don't know if I can do it anymore," she admitted anyway, because it was him and because they had said it a million times before — and then a million times after, they would get up the next morning and do it again. It was just how it worked. Their greatest dream had become a nightmare they couldn't escape.

"You might not have to." Shadows passed across Ezra's drawn features — features which Ruby knew weren't just caused by their perpetual discontent. He avoided her gaze, scraping a hand over his face and pinching the bridge of his nose.

Ruby frowned, sitting forward in her chair and tugging his wrist away so that she could see his face again. His skin felt somehow both hot and cold, soft and rough in her palm. "What do you mean?"

"I...." Ezra chewed at his lip, looking anywhere but at her. "I did something stupid today."

She groaned. "Not another groupie."

He didn't laugh as he usually would, his face remaining hewn from stone, and dread curdled in Ruby's stomach. He always laughed at her jokes. Even the ones that weren't funny.

"What?" she asked. "What did you do?"

"After the meeting." His jaw clenched, a muscle tensing beneath a dark shadow of stubble that would no doubt be shaved tomorrow. Just as it was every day. For the fans. They wouldn't like it if he looked older, more unkempt. It wasn't the right "image."

Ruby's dread intensified as his words finally resonated. The meeting. They'd had a meeting with their team today, another arbitrary rattling off of rules and decisions the band had no say in: what they would do next, where they would go, how they would sing their songs and treat the fans and sell themselves to the public with false relationships and planned appearances that were supposed to look candid. It had been the final straw for her. Confirmation that when her contract was up in two years, she would take a much-needed hiatus. Find out who she was without a dozen different people heckling her with power-points about who she *should* be.

She knew Ezra had hated it, too. It had ruined his last relationship and the hope of any future ones. They would lose fans — Mason, Fusion's company director and head of management, had claimed — if he was seen kissing a man. Crazed teenage girls liked to believe their idols were obtainable, and despite their rock sounds brimming with adult content, they were nothing if not idolised by teens. Well, Ezra was idolised; many of them didn't like Ruby. She didn't follow all of the conventions of a popular musician despite Fusion's attempt to change her, especially since she had curves in all the wrong places and refused to slim down. That, and she was now believed to have stolen the "future husband" from millions of teenage girls. In the last few months alone, she had been the target of countless death threats, and with some of them arriving in dressing rooms and hotel suites, Cerys believed a stalker was at play. Ruby tried not to think anything of it, though they had also managed to get her last phone number somehow and had sent text messages that made Ruby feel sick.

But if Ezra had blown up about it all today, or if he had hinted towards the fact that he and Ruby wanted out….

"*What?*" Ruby gulped, voice hoarse and throat dry. "After the meeting, *what?*"

"I talked to Mason in his office," he said. Ruby held her breath, praying he was not about to say what she thought he was. "I told him that things can't go on as they are. I told him that you almost passed out on stage last week, that they're running us into the ground and it's not right."

She squeezed her eyes closed, though it did nothing to make her feel better. She *had* almost passed out. Stress had left her without an appetite, so she wasn't eating as much as she should. With that and the two hours of sleep she got — if she was lucky — each night along with the anxiety of crowds always screaming at her and the constant and inescapable need to paste on a smile and be *Ruby Bright, lead singer of Gen Y*, it was no wonder her body had given out on her. At the end of the set, with dizziness engulfing her, she had almost fallen off stage and into the crowd. It was Ezra who'd pulled her back, cutting the gig short and hauling her backstage to get medical attention.

Exhaustion and a lack of iron spurred on by her period had been the diagnosis. The treatment had been a large bottle of water, a few protein bars, iron tablets, and another show the next day. And the next, and the next, and the next. None of it had stopped her from feeling unsteady on her feet every time she stood. Perhaps that would never go away now. Perhaps once she had stopped listening to her body, it had stopped listening to her, and the two would continue on with this long-distance relationship that could only ever end in disconnect.

"And what did he say?" Ruby could guess the answer. *The show must go on. No pain no gain.* All of the other toxic positivity quotes one could find stamped on graphic tees in Primark. They were all Mason's favourite way of brushing them under the rug and making sure they continued to rake in the money.

"He said this is what I signed up for, and if I want to be a rock star, I'll have to deal with it." Ezra's fingers flexed with anger, and Ruby took hold of them quickly to calm him down, drawing soothing circles around his knuckles. "I couldn't help it, Rubes. I exploded. I can't do it anymore. I can't watch them do it to *you*. I told him that if he didn't step up and fix things, we'd come clean to the press about everything. The lying, the mistreatment, pushing us to the brink of exhaustion, making us hide our relationships, withholding our earnings. *All* of it."

"Ezra." It was the only thing Ruby could manage to say with her heart hammering against her ribs so violently.

"*Something* has to change."

"And will it? Because I can't imagine Mason responding well to blackmail." Her voice quaked, still recovering from the show. Just another thing pushed to the point of breaking. Another thing Fusion relied on, but not enough to give a toss about. There would be nothing of her left soon.

Ezra grimaced and leaned back, letting go of Ruby's hand to rake his fingers through his hair again. "Yeah, well... he didn't. He threatened me. Said he could break us *like that*." A click of his fingers. Ruby could imagine Mason's wide thumb and ring-littered forefinger performing the same gesture. "I said I didn't care. Let him break us. At least then we'll be free."

Ruby groaned. "You should have *talked* to me about this before you went in there, guns blazing. We agreed we'd figure it out together."

"I didn't mean for it to happen. I didn't plan it. I just lost my head after that stupid fucking meeting and everything just… came out."

She couldn't blame him for it. Ruby wished she was stronger, too. Strong enough to speak out. But she also knew that it took more than strength in this industry, especially when she was locked into a contract for a multimillion-pound company. She had seen other clients endure the same hardships, but she had also seen them leave when their contract was up with enough money and respect to be able to take a long break. To be free again. Maybe even return to the charts under new management years later, well-rested and sounding better than ever.

That was just how it was supposed to be.

But now Ezra had broken all the rules.

Ruby sighed her frustration, bringing her knees to her chest and contemplating what would be next. At best, a slap on the wrist. At worst, their lives made a hundred times worse than they already were, with stricter regimens as a reminder that they weren't the ones in control here. Whenever they pushed, Fusion always pushed back with their teeth bared and claws sharpened. Ruby had learned this the hard way when she had come into her fame as a naïve twenty-five-year-old who still had a shred of integrity. They had made sure to snuff that out quickly.

"Don't be mad at me," Ezra whispered, eyes puppy-dog soft as he twirled a finger through Ruby's dark waves.

"I'm not mad at you." It was the truth. Ruby was frightened and exhausted, but she couldn't blame Ezra for reaching his breaking point. God knows she had reached hers. "I just… I can't see an end to this. Can you?"

He shook his head and pulled her close. She fell into him, burrowing her head into his warm chest and inhaling the stale scent of whiskey, sweat-mingled cologne, and cigarettes. The closest thing she had to home. She couldn't imagine ever getting through this without him. At least they were in it together, even if it was just as painful to watch Ezra suffer too.

After a few moments of nothing but the bus's purr and the din downstairs, he murmured, "Maybe we *should* come clean to the press. Mason can ruin our careers, but at least we'd finally be free."

"And then what?" Ruby asked. "I can't see you as a plumber or a teacher or a lawyer."

Ezra snorted. "We'd figure it out. Maybe I have a hidden talent somewhere."

She wished she could believe it. It was why she was still here. She couldn't go back to… *noth-*

ing. She couldn't let her family do the same. She'd bought her Aunt Fiona a house the first time she'd gotten a dreg of her earnings, leaving her comfortable enough that she was able to start a family with her husband — a life Ruby never had, and she wasn't going to pull that rug from under her aunt. She wasn't going back to standing behind a cash register in Asda either.

"We're going to be okay," said Ezra. "It's you and me against the world, yeah?"

"Yeah." Ruby smiled and let Ezra's breath lull her into sleep. For hours they stayed there… until the party downstairs guttered out and the sky paled with morning — and the tour bus careened off the road somewhere along the M1 motorway.

It was the lurch that woke Ruby. She didn't have time to grip onto anything, though she could feel Ezra gripping her, his fingers bunching in her jumper. And then honking, and the world tumbling upside down, and them being thrown apart as they were battered from all sides. Screams. Agonising pain. Was she upside down? She didn't have time to find out. They kept going, kept hurtling towards a place that seemed to have no finish line.

Ezra, she wanted to shout, but her breath was torn from her.

Ruby lost Ezra after that. She lost everything — enslaved by darkness offering no reprieve.

When she woke in the hospital days later with bruised ribs and a broken arm, Ezra was still gone.

CHAPTER ONE

Everything that Ruby had seen of Cumbria so far was tainted by black-tinted windows and sharp pains shooting through her ribcage. She hadn't been able to decide yet if the latter were a result of the accident itself or what she had lost in it. Absently, she stared out onto rolling fields and many, many lakes, wondering how she was going to spend the foreseeable future in the middle of nowhere without going mad. One prison swapped for another, only this one was very colourless and very cold and very Ezra-less — much like the rest of the world since she'd woken in the hospital.

She missed him. She couldn't bear how much she missed him. So much of her felt numb still, as though unconsciousness had never really released its clawing grip on her after the crash. Even as Cerys rattled off information about cancelling the tour, through a phone she had been warned would be confiscated soon, Ruby was barely listening. It felt like being trapped underwater, the surface just unreachable and covered with a sheet of ice. Without Ezra, she didn't think she'd want to break through it anyway. It was easier this way, wrapped in grief, with nothing able to touch her but the distant aches and pains of supposed recovery.

"Ruby?" Cerys's voice sounded wary — an unusual occurrence for Ruby's ruthless manager.

"Yes?" Ruby's voice was hoarse from what little speaking she had done, sounding alien to her ears. She wondered if Cerys was about to prescribe her another diet of honey and lemon tea to soothe it for when all of this would be over and she would make her big comeback. Apparently, having her tour bus crash, killing half of the band's road crew *and* their guitar player and drummer, had not been reason enough for Ruby to be released from her contract. Cerys wanted her to spend the next two years pursuing a solo career. *When you're ready and all of this is settled, of course*, which was just code for when Fusion began to see the loss of earnings.

"You're going to be okay, you know?" Cerys said, voice light and unsure as they treaded this foreign territory. Their friendship had been based on ignoring all of the awful things before — Cerys making sure Ruby ate and slept and took care of herself but never acknowledging why those things were impossible to do in the first place. "They'll catch your crazy stalker. I'll make sure of it."

Ruby hardly believed that Cerys held any bearing over Scotland Yard's power to find the person who everyone assumed was behind the crash after realising the attack was targeted. A stolen car, a runaway driver, and a threatening letter, delivered to Ruby's hospital room shortly after, had been the evidence.

Ruby closed her eyes against memories she didn't want to see, letting the car rock her until she felt drowsy. "I know."

"And you'll write while you're there?"

Ruby hadn't been able to pick up a pen since the crash, and not just because of her broken right arm, now pinned in a stiff white cast, but she nodded and hummed her agreement anyway. As long as she kept writing music, kept being profitable. As long as she was still Ruby Bright, even when there was no Gen Y to sing with anymore.

"All right. I know it's easier said than done, but just enjoy the time away, yeah? You deserve it." The way Cerys crooned "*yeah*" as "*yah*" grated on Ruby when it never had before, as though she was a Californian reality star rather than a woman born in Leeds, England. "Listen, I've got to go but I love you, babe, and I'll see you soon, okay?"

"'Kay. Bye."

As she hung up, Ruby's sigh cleaved through the taut silence of the car. The officer who was driving, a tall, thirty-something man who had introduced himself as "Officer Liam Halstead but just Liam is fine," glanced over his shoulder for just a moment. His lips spread into an easy, amicable grin, an attempt at reassurance. Somehow, that grin reminded Ruby of Ezra, and the pain ricocheted all over again, swiftly chased by the void swallowing her.

"Time to turn off your phone, Ruby," Liam

said.

She did, glad to see the back of hundreds of unopened text messages and Twitter DMs. At least now she had an excuse not to answer them. She handed the phone to the woman in the passenger seat, one of Fusion's hired security team members who had introduced herself as Claire, and watched as she slid it into the glove compartment.

It took another hour for the snaking tree-lined lanes to be swapped for uneven gravel and spongy soil. A house came into view not long after, grey-bricked and red-doored. The car slowed to a stop, and a small pang of distaste cut through Ruby's numbness.

For a so-called "safe house," it didn't look very safe.

The buildings were old, a stable and outdoor shed flanking the crumbling farmhouse on either side. Even the fence lining the large expanse of land was crooked and low, though there were plenty of trees sequestering the area in all directions. By the smoking chimney on the roof of the main house, a lonely weathervane pirouetted in the wind, screeching rustily as though forced against its will.

Ruby didn't know if she would be able to manage in a place like this. It was so… ramshackle. Drab. Isolated.

Robotically, she unfastened her seatbelt and let Liam open the door for her. As she stepped out, her Gucci leather boots sank into a murky puddle, leaving her jeans splattered with dirt. She rolled her eyes, and then her attention was snapped to the creaking of a door.

A blonde woman emerged from the main house, a black Labrador racing out with her. The latter sprang up onto Ruby, sullying her houndstooth-patterned coat with dirty paw prints and nearly knocking her back into the car. It left her tender rib cage singing with pain, and she let out an *Oof!* as she fought to be free.

"Flint!" the woman scolded, prying the dog away by its blue collar. Unfazed, the dog only wagged its tail and raced off to chase a band of pigeons flapping out of the tall shrubs. "You'll have to excuse him. He's only boisterous around new people."

Her accent was lilting, Irish, but nothing else about her appeared quite as soft and musical. Though Ruby knew it was silly and outdated, she was just surprised the owner was a woman. When Liam had informed her that they were headed to a farmhouse in the Lake District, where she would live with just him, the three security guards gathered on the gravel now, and the land's owner, she'd imagined the farmers she'd grown up around in Peterborough: grumpy old men with shotguns at the ready and pipes jutting from their mouths.

But the woman was not old, though judging by the deeply-set knit of her brows and stiff, square jaw, Ruby suspected she might have been a little bit grumpy. She couldn't have been more than six or seven years older than Ruby herself, with faint lines bracketing a thinly-pressed mouth and piercing green eyes that Ruby couldn't quite meet.

"It's fine," Ruby lied finally, brushing down her coat with her good hand and clearing her throat.

"Ruby, this is Shea O'Connor." Liam's brown eyes flickered warmly to Shea as he introduced her in a way that could only mean they had known each other a while. "She owns the farmland here and she's a retired protection officer herself, so you're in good hands."

Retired? How could she have retired when she looked younger than the majority of the officers surrounding her?

Shea wiped her palms on her grubby, tattered jeans and then extended a hand. Her eyes flicked to Ruby's feet and her brows lifted. "Hope you brought your Wellies."

Ruby had done no such thing. She didn't even own Wellington boots, though she didn't say so as she shook Shea's hand with little enthusiasm.

"Don't overwhelm me with too much conversation." Shea's features danced with light-hearted taunting and Ruby began to suspect that she wouldn't like the woman very much. "I'll show you around, shall I?"

Ruby nodded and followed warily. Shea pointed to the stable first.

"Horses are in there. They'll need mucking out once a day and fed twice, grain and hay.

Same goes for their water buckets. The pigsty and chicken coop are just behind the house."

Shea motioned over her shoulder, guiding Ruby down the side of the farmhouse, through squelching mud and trampled grass, to a large expanse of land. Horses grazed in the field beyond, and the black Labrador ran in maniacal circles until he made Ruby dizzy. She gazed at the scenery without interest, still protected by that unfeeling bubble she had trapped herself in. Shea's words were barely registering at all — until Shea started telling her how to care for the pigs and keep the sty clean, and then Ruby realised that she was being given instructions rather than a simple tour.

"Hang on," she uttered, interrupting something Shea was saying about chickens mid-sentence. "Why do I need to know all of this?"

Shea frowned, clamping her lips together as though trying to suppress her amusement. "Excuse me?"

"I'm not here as a free farmhand."

"Ah, I see." Shea took a step closer, the ends of her blonde hair curling into her neck. Ruby caught the smell of hay and earth wafting from her. "Our pop star planned to laze about and enjoy a free holiday, did she?"

An unexpected spark of anger roared to life in Ruby. The first real thing she had felt in two weeks. "I'm not here to *work.* I'm here because my life is in danger."

"I'm well aware of that. But I'm offering this

place as your sanctuary. I expect the favour to be returned with a little bit of help around the farm. Most people are quite happy to oblige."

"I'm not most people." Ruby didn't mean for it to sound the way she did; like she thought she was special, more important. Perhaps a few years of being idolised by strangers had gone to her head more than she'd realised.

With a high-pitched whistle, Shea hooked her fingers through her belt loops and rocked back on her heels. "This is why I stopped working with the rich and famous, Liam."

Liam chuckled, and Ruby's cheeks burned. Were they *laughing* at her? "Go easy on her, Shea. She's been through the wringer."

"Haven't we all?" Shea studied Ruby again coolly, and Ruby fought not to squirm. And then the blonde woman stepped away, kicking the loose flagstones at her feet. "You'll not live the life of luxury here, love. If you wanted that, you should have stayed in London. The rules are simple and they're non-negotiable. Help out where you can or find someone else to help you."

Ruby narrowed her eyes. "I have a broken *arm*."

"The other one still looks intact. Capable of holding a trowel and pouring chicken feed, I'd bet."

Ruby shook her head, dumbfounded by the woman's brusqueness. As though she hadn't been through enough, she had to put up with being scolded like a servant as well. Still, she didn't have the energy to argue, and her response came out sounding flat. "I'd like to see my room now, please."

Shea grinned sardonically and opened the back door: an arched slab of chipped mahogany and stained glass. And then, with a flourish of her hand, she bowed dramatically. "This way, Your Excellency. I hope you're not allergic to dust."

* * *

"Don't you think it's weird that they're using their own security company for this?" Shea questioned, drawing back the yellowing, lace curtains to peek at the two officers wandering the perimeter. They had introduced themselves as Eric and Leona shortly after Ruby had retired to her room, and while Shea had been keeping them fed and watered with sandwiches and cups of tea all afternoon, she didn't like them.

Not like she liked Liam, anyway. It felt like a divide, with him in his navy-blue uniform and them in black blazers. The other officer, who had made camp in the security quarters behind the abandoned barn, worked with them too. Claire. She had been even more stone-faced than the others, and making conversation with her had been like drawing blood from a stone.

In the window's reflection, Shea caught the shrug of Liam's shoulders and turned back to him. He leaned on the kitchen counter, sipping his coffee from an oversized mug and feeding

Flint diced carrots and potatoes from the chopping board when he thought Shea wasn't looking.

"I suppose our lot are spread thin, what with all the cutbacks. Plus, she's an international celebrity and we have no idea what kind of threat we're dealing with. They're used to taking care of fancy actors. In fact, they're probably far more trained in it all than we ever were."

Shea scowled, thinking it highly unlikely. She returned to the stew simmering on the stove and stirred through the thick gravy with a ladle. "Right. I keep forgetting we have royalty in our midst."

"No you don't," Liam smirked. "Everyone knows *Ruby Bright*."

Shea didn't. Perhaps she might have been subjected to the occasional Gen Y song on the radio, but she hadn't bothered to research the pop star before her arrival and hadn't even known what she'd looked like. The solemn-faced, curvy woman who had emerged from Liam's car was most definitely not what Shea had expected, anyway, though the fancy clothes and entitled attitude came closer. But it seemed false somehow, as though she was wearing an outfit that didn't quite fit, a normal — albeit ridiculously good-looking — person pretending to be something more.

"You know I don't have the patience for all of that crap," Shea dismissed with a wave of her hand, sprinkling a generous amount of salt and pepper and then turning off the hob. "She might be famous out there, but in this house, she'll be treated like the rest of us."

"Shea." Liam's fingers curled gently around the well-toned muscle of her upper arm, his almond eyes hardening with an authority he rarely showed in front of Shea. They were equals, regardless of whether Shea had retired. Friends. They had to be when they spent most of their days trapped here, though there were times — miserable, dull times — when Liam wasn't assigned to this house. "Be careful with her. She's had it really rough."

"She's not made of glass, Liam," Shea replied, pursing her lips as she pulled away from his grasp. "And she's no different from anyone else who walks through these doors. We've all been through something. If she wanted to be mollycoddled, she came to the wrong place."

Liam sighed but didn't argue, having long since grown used to Shea's stubbornness. It was who she had always been. Who she *had* to be for so many reasons. That wasn't going to change because a celebrity lived here now.

"If you want to make yourself useful, get the loaf out of the bread bin. And then you can go and see if *Her Highness* will be joining us for dinner," she ordered, rising on her tiptoes to collect a stack of chipped china bowls. They were so old now that the delicate blue pattern was faded and scratched but, like most things in this house, Shea couldn't bring herself to replace them. Her mother's memory still lived in them, in everything here, they were the only thing Shea had left of her now.

"Yes, ma'am," Liam muttered with a famil-iarity Shea hadn't shared with anyone else for a long time. Not that she minded. Being alone here with her animals was rewarding enough and kept her so busy that she rarely had time to feel lonely. Besides, sometimes she ended up getting along with the clients she offered out the house to — another way in which she had followed in her mother's footsteps after retiring from the service. This place had always been a safe house, and one of the first ones Shea herself had after moving from Ireland. It deserved to stay that way.

As she buttered the seeded bread haphaz-ardly, Liam returned from the corridor with a brooding Ruby following behind. Her dark curls had been piled into a tousled updo, eyes bleary with sleep, and Shea fought the urge to scoff. "Enjoy your afternoon snooze, love?"

"Your mattress is lumpy," was all that Ruby said as she took her place at the dining table.

"Oh, is it? I'll have that replaced for you immediately, madam, so you can sit on your arse more comfortably." Shea's voice dripped with sar-casm as she rolled her eyes and ladled the stew out into three bowls. There was plenty for the others when they changed shifts. Shea always found her-self with too many leftovers when it came to the brief intermissions between visitors since she was so used to cooking for a full house now.

Ignoring the musician's glare, she placed the

bowls of stew and the plate of bread on the table and took a seat beside Liam. Liam cast her another reprimanding look as he picked up his spoon and dug in.

Ruby didn't seem quite as enthusiastic about the food. She poked a lump of beef around with her spoon, eyeing it as though Shea had served her a bowl of Flint's turds and not a perfectly hearty meal.

"Is the cooking not up to your standards, either?" asked Shea, mopping up the gravy with the crust of her bread and watching Ruby expectantly. She was already at her wit's end with the woman. She never usually minded going out of her way to host people in need of a secure, hidden place, quite happy to stay out of their way so long as they helped out where they could and showed at least a flicker of appreciation for Shea's efforts. But this one hadn't done any of those things yet — and didn't look as though she planned to. She'd been spoiled by a life of luxury and had left her manners in London, it seemed.

"What is it?" Ruby spooned out a carrot and nibbled at it warily.

"Rabbit."

Ruby's gaze flicked up in alarm, and Shea stifled her laugh behind another mouthful of bread.

"It's beef stew. Don't tell me you've never had stew."

"It's good stew," Liam added through a

mouthful of bread. He'd already demolished half of his bowl and would no doubt go in for seconds. Shea always knew to make extra for that reason alone.

"I'm not all that hungry." Ruby abandoned her spoon and picked up a piece of bread instead.

With a scowl, Shea replied, "If you'd rather make your own meals, you're most welcome to."

"*Shea*," Liam chided, and then to Ruby, softly: "You don't have to eat the stew if you don't want to, but you should eat *something*."

With a ragged sigh, Ruby rose from her chair, the wooden legs scraping against fifty-year-old tiles. From the floor, Flint rose with her, probably waiting for his share of the scraps. "I think I'm going to have an early night, actually. Thank you for the... stew."

Shea was too insulted to respond — even more so when Flint followed the woman out of the kitchen. Flint, the dog Shea fed and cared for and walked every day. *Traitorous mutt.*

When the door closed behind them, Liam flashed her another terse glance of disapproval. "Would it kill you to be a little bit more pleasant?"

"Oh, please," Shea scoffed, devouring the rest of her meal so that she wouldn't have to look at him. Maybe she *had* been a little bit harsh considering she didn't know the ins and outs of Ruby's story, but that was who she'd always been, and anyone close to her understood that. It just seemed that haughty pop stars dragged it out of her more intensely. "Stop kissing her arse and help me wash up."

Liam rolled his eyes but obeyed, collecting the bowls from the table and placing them by the sink. "You're a bloody irritating woman, Shea O'Connor."

She smirked. "And you're stuck with me. Lucky you."

CHAPTER TWO

Ruby awoke at dawn with the rooster, though it had not been the jarring crows that had tugged her from sleep. She'd been dreaming again. Of Ezra and the crash and a faceless shadow chasing her wherever she went. It left her drenched in sweat, her pulse a frantic thrum rushing through her blood.

Flint, who had been lying peacefully at her feet all night, rose and stretched before making his way over to her and curling into her side. She tried to go back to sleep at first, finding comfort in the dog's soft fur and faithful presence, but with the noise and the panic and her thoughts no longer something she could lock away, it soon became clear that that wasn't going to happen. The awful, cheap mattress didn't help, either, leaving her ribs aching even more than they had yesterday. Eventually, she took a shower and, when that wasn't enough to lull her back into that numbness she had been so content in, she wandered the house.

The floorboards creaked with her footsteps, and she treaded carefully until she found a bedroom door open. Shea must have already gotten up. When she glimpsed through the window though, she only saw Liam and Leona chatting outside, warming their hands with mugs of coffee.

The morning's shadows followed Ruby through the farmhouse as she explored without the disturbance of Shea rattling off duties and rules. She had barely been focusing yesterday, only wanting a place to escape to, lumpy mattress be damned. Now, she ran her fingers across dust-caked shelves and tattered book spines, corduroy-clothed armchairs and old, fragile ornaments that reminded Ruby of her grandma's house. The living room barely looked touched, though there was a television and a fireplace, which Ruby would have made the most of if she had the privacy.

That wasn't what she was drawn to though: a grand piano and stool were pushed up to the far wall, gathering dust. Ruby inched towards it as though it was a wild animal that might bite. In the end, she couldn't help but lift the fallboard and trace the ivory keys, her touch light enough to keep them from making a noise. She hadn't touched an instrument since the crash. She hadn't even been able to bring her guitar here with her, though she could have. But it all reminded her too much of Ezra, and only silence felt the right soundtrack to her grief. It felt like a betrayal to play without him, even if she only had the one good arm to do it with.

With that in mind, she lowered the cover again and closed her eyes against the sudden burning of oncoming tears.

No.

But her brain wanted to replay her last moments with him on that tour bus before she'd fallen asleep in his arms. *It's you and me against the world.*

Now it was just Ruby, and Ruby didn't know what to do with that. Especially now, with nothing to distract her. At least if she was back in London, management wouldn't give her time to grieve. She would keep working, keep being Ruby Bright. A curse before, but now a distraction she found herself needing. And if not London, she would have gone home to her aunt.

God, she missed her aunt and her cousins, her family.

Restless with the need to keep moving, to stop thinking, Ruby's feet took her out of the farmhouse and onto the dirt. She was greeted by the low snorts of the pigs and the clucking of the chickens. Beyond the yard, the fields were empty save for Flint chasing a gaggle of geese who must have lost their way, the sky a surreal, mottled purple and dripping with dark clouds. Ruby found herself walking towards the stables to the horses. She'd always loved them as a child until her parents couldn't afford to pay for the riding lessons anymore.

Ruby shifted outside the door. It was open already, but she saw no sign of Shea anywhere. She felt eyes on her back, though, and turned to find Liam waving at her from the driveway. "Morning, Ruby."

Ruby forced a shaky smile and then stepped

inside. The smell of hay was familiar and comforting somehow. The nearest horse, a tall chestnut-brown with a black mane, watched her with a beady eye.

"Hello," she whispered, reaching out carefully. When the horse made no move, she ran a gentle hand down from between its ears to its muzzle, trying not to notice the trembling of her fingers as she did. "You're friendly."

After a few moments, she stopped to hug herself, the stiffness of her cast a shield against her ribs. She needed it to keep herself from falling apart.

It wasn't enough.

Her mind was still racing, still replaying that night. She imagined Ezra here with her now, how much easier it would be. And then she remembered that she would never see him again, and it was a constant, relentless pattern of wishing he was here and then being reminded of the harsh reality that he never would be again.

Because of her. Because of some crazed stalker who had wanted to destroy Ruby. Who probably still did. But they had destroyed Ezra instead.

She couldn't stand here and think about it a moment longer. She needed a distraction. She needed to be busy.

So she called Liam to take the horses onto the field and got to work.

✻ ✻ ✻

Shea was certain that she was hallucinating when she arrived home from a grocery run to find Ruby Bright mucking out her stable. Too shocked to even unload the bags, she got out of her Jeep with her keys rattling in her hands, kicking up hay as she reached the open door. She leaned against the splintering frame wordlessly and watched for a few moments.

Ruby was doing a terrible job, straw caking her jeans and the rest of the stables, too, as she struggled to shovel with her one good hand. Still, she was doing it and that was something.

"Not a bad job for a pop star," Shea commented finally, causing Ruby to halt her work and turn. "I reckon a proper day's work'll do you good."

A light sheen of sweat clung to Ruby's forehead, cheeks rosy and hair a tangled mess fighting to get free of its braid. She scowled at Shea's words, resting the shovel against the gate and blowing baby hairs from her face. "I'm not a pop star."

"No?" Shea's brow arched in amusement.

"No."

"Who let the horses out?" Sudden images of Ruby letting them run free, never to be seen again, ran through her mind.

"Liam," Ruby said, putting Shea's mind at ease. Liam was as well acquainted with the horses as Shea by now.

"Okay." She tried not to hide the fact that she was impressed, though she was — just slightly. It would save her the graft of having to do it herself later, along with everything else it took to maintain a farm on her own. "Good. I'll unload the shopping and then I'll help you out."

"I don't need your help," Ruby answered indignantly, starting up her haphazard shovelling again. "I'd rather do it alone."

So it seemed the brattiness hadn't disappeared completely. Shea was half-glad. She might have had to call for assistance if Ruby continued to be helpful and decent.

"Suit yourself." Shrugging, Shea twirled her keys around her index finger. "Lunch is at twelve. Are you too good for sandwiches, too?"

Ruby's nostrils flared, and she stabbed at the hay with more aggression than she had a moment ago. "Sandwiches are fine."

"Grand. After that, you can make a start on the pigs." Shea left it at that, wandering back to the car to unload her shopping. If Ruby wanted to work alone, Shea would make sure she had plenty to do.

❋ ❋ ❋

After three days of non-stop work, Ruby had more than earned her keep at the farm. She woke at four o'clock every morning with Flint pinning her down, showered after ten minutes of probing him to move, and went to the stable before the pain could touch her. Emotional pain, anyway. Working hadn't staved off her physical pain, with her ribs throbbing from the mechanical movements of handling wheelbarrows and large shovels, all one-handedly.

She didn't care about that, though. She'd soon learned that it was easier to deal with the ache of her ribs than the one threatening to consume her just behind them. And today, she would take any distraction she could get.

It had been a rough night of tossing and turning and thinking too much. Thinking about the stalker she'd dismissed so easily before the crash. Missing Ezra. The last conversation they'd had. Wondering if she owed it to her best friend to do what he'd wanted and come clean about the mistreatment they'd faced from Fusion. It was too quiet here, even when the birds sang. Even with Shea sending sardonic quips her way. Even with Liam singing under his breath when he took his coffee break. Perhaps she'd been subjected to constant noise and screams and music for so long that she no longer knew how to have it any other way. Her most tranquil moments after gigs had still come with the whirring of a tour bus, always moving, always somewhere to be and something to do.

Now she had nothing. No Ezra, no noise, no purpose. It was too easy to drown in the sorrow here. Too easy to wonder if she even knew who she was without it all.

So she pushed through the agonising twinges in her ribs and fought against the restrictions of her cast as she worked on the farm that day. She didn't stop for lunch, even when Shea nagged that she needed to eat. She didn't stop for dinner, either; hadn't even realised that it was going dark until her name was called and she lifted her gaze, from the heap of logs she was currently trying to shift from the backyard, to find Shea standing with her hands on her hips in the doorway.

"What?" Ruby could barely rasp out the word, heart pounding in her ears and sweat trickling down the back of her neck. It was how she felt after performing. Drained, empty, exhausted, as though she'd given every bit of herself she could. But it wasn't enough. She could still feel the emotions teetering behind her like a shadow, ready to throw her to the ground if she let them come near.

"The day's over. You've done enough. Come and eat something," Shea said.

"When it gets dark." Ruby bent over again and tried not to sway with the sudden head rush. Nausea had wrung her stomach dry long ago, and her mouth felt like sandpaper tainted with a bitter taste she couldn't name.

"No," Shea ordered, stepping out. The loose flagstones popped beneath her weight. "*Now*."

"I'm helping as you asked. Now you don't want me to?"

"It's all or nothing with you, isn't it?" Shea

huffed. "You're going to collapse if you carry on like that."

Wouldn't be the first time. Only then Ezra had been there to keep her from falling. He wasn't here now. Nobody was here now. "I'm fine."

"Well, I'm not. I can't afford to get sued when you end up dead on my land."

She scoffed at that, though it took more energy than she had and ended up more of a groan. "You're all heart."

"*Ruby*." It was the first time Ruby had heard her name on Shea's tongue, and the sharpness of it was enough to stop Ruby in her tracks. She glanced up, finding lines etched in Shea's forehead, green eyes cold as frosted grass in winter. "Get in the fecking house before I drag you in!"

Ruby somehow didn't doubt that Shea would do it, too.

The log dropped from Ruby's blistered hand and clattered back to the pile. She took a breath, dabbing her sweat-slick forehead with the hem of her jumper. Her knees felt ready to give under her weight, and she took slow, careful steps into the house, guided by a frowning Shea. She didn't miss the clicking of the locks and bolts when the door slammed shut.

Flint was there to greet her, but Ruby didn't have the energy to give him the attention he pined for at her feet. Instead, she collapsed into a chair at the dining table, where a mammoth bowl of pasta had already been laid out on a table mat.

"Eat," Shea ordered, resting against the counter with her arms crossed expectantly.

"Are you going to stand there and watch me?"

"Yes."

Ruby sighed and speared a tomato-sauce-drenched pasta shell with her fork, but realised when she tried to chew it that her mouth was too dry and she almost gagged. She glugged down the glass of water Shea had set out for her and tried again, stomach grumbling with the first nutrition it had gotten all day.

Seemingly content that she was eating, Shea sat in the chair opposite, resting her elbows against the table. "You're not doing this again tomorrow. You can take a break."

Ruby wrinkled her nose petulantly. "What happened to 'help out or find someone else to help you'?"

"What happened to 'I'm not here to work'?" Shea retorted.

Huffing, Ruby pushed her plate away to run a hand over her face. After a few meagre bites, she was bloated. Her stomach couldn't handle being starved one moment and full the next, and nothing tasted the way it used to. "I need the distraction."

"There's a difference between distraction and punishing yourself." Shea shoved the plate back to Ruby, but Ruby had frozen at Shea's words, heat creeping up her neck and her stomach twisting with something oily.

Punishing herself? Is that what she was doing? It hadn't felt that way, but....

"I don't know what you're talking about."

"Yes, you do," Shea said knowingly. "I've seen plenty of different walks of life in this house. Criminals. Victims. People who have something to hide from and people who are trying to hide from themselves. I know what it looks like when someone is trying to destroy themselves. What you did today was stupid and unhealthy and it could have gotten you seriously injured. When you realise that, you can start up with the usual chores again. Until then, you'll have to find another 'distraction.'"

"Are you this kind to all your guests?" Ruby snapped, white-hot anger beginning to bubble beneath her skin. She was tired of this. Tired of everything. Tired of being told how to act and how to cope, tired of being trapped in an unfamiliar place when she should be with Ezra on the tour bus. She would have endured all of the late nights and anxiety and fatigue if it meant just being back with Ezra on that damned tour bus.

Shea examined her steadily, eyes narrowing. "It's not about kindness. That's not my job."

"What *is* your job? Because a retired cop living on a rundown farm is hardly a success story, is it? And it definitely doesn't give you the right to tell me what to do and how to feel or make snap judgements about who I am."

Ruby didn't wait for Shea's reaction after the outburst, instead leaving the table and marching to her bedroom without a second look back. Flint followed on her heels, sidling up to her when she shut the door and collapsed onto her bed. She didn't even have the energy for a shower. She didn't have the energy for anything.

The exhaustion at least kept her nightmares at bay that night.

CHAPTER THREE

"There was a lot of slamming doors last night." Accusation sharpened Liam's voice as he crossed his arms over his chest. "I heard them from out here."

Coming to a halt, Shea pulled out her earbuds and tried to catch her breath. Sweat dripped from her hairline and trickled down her spine, her T-shirt clinging to her sticky skin. She hadn't planned a five-kilometre run at the break of dawn, but her muscles had been knotted with tension leftover from her argument with Ruby the night before, and she'd needed a release. She'd be paying for it later, mind, and could already feel the muscles in her ruined back twinging with that promise.

"The woman's bloody impossible," she ranted, bracing her palm against the uneven stone of the farmhouse and trying to ignore the slight tendril of guilt curling in her chest. Shea had been harsh on Ruby — *again*. But the woman had been hellbent on pushing herself to the brink of exhaustion yesterday, and Shea couldn't have a liability on her hands. She offered out this house to protect people that needed it, not watch them destroy themselves.

"Is she?" Liam cocked an eyebrow, and Shea glowered. He was too nice. He saw the good in people. She'd never had that kind of empathy.

Or maybe she had. Maybe empathy wasn't the problem. Maybe Ruby got under Shea's skin so easily because Shea saw too much of herself. That grief, the way she was so willing to be consumed by it, to punish herself for it.

It wasn't the same. They hadn't lived the same experiences. Shea would never be a bloody entitled pop star with too much money in her bank account. But Shea still remembered how her own anger and self-loathing had blazed after the accident. How it had taken months, years, to get to where she was now: running the farm; trying to quell any bitterness about not being able to return to her old job; refusing to think of people who had once meant everything to her. Ruby was just an unwelcome reminder, a grotesque reflection, and Shea didn't need it.

She gritted her teeth against Liam's disbelief, toeing a loose stone in the gravel to distract herself. "Oh, come on, Liam. Don't act like *I'm* the problem."

"She's grieving. Nobody in her position deserves to be treated the way you're treating her. You should understand that better than anyone."

Shea did understand it. She'd gone through her own pain alone; had shut herself off from Liam and her dad and anyone else who tried to reach out. But that was different. She had to keep reminding herself of that. "You saw how she was yesterday. She almost pushed herself to the brink of collapse. Maybe she needs some tough love."

"Tough love is a load of shit and you know it," he scoffed. "Do you even know what happened to her?"

At a loss, Shea shook her head. She'd glimpsed the case file over Liam's shoulder, and the email from the head of witness protection, and Shea's old boss had told her plenty when assigning the farmhouse. Ruby Bright was a highly important person in need of the highest security possible because of a suspected threat to her life, most likely in the form of a crazed stalker. Her injuries were from some sort of targeted road accident.

Liam pressed his lips together impatiently, eyes dark in the streaked shadows of the rising sun. "It's time you started reading the news."

"I know enough," she spat, not one to enjoy feeling out of the loop. "A stalker, right? She was in a car accident, and they think that the two things were linked."

"That's half of it." He nodded. "It wasn't a car accident, Shea. It was the tour bus that crashed. And it wasn't just Ruby caught up in it. She lost two of her bandmates. Her *boyfriend*. Whoever it was left death threats while she was recovering in hospital."

"Right." It was hard for Shea to swallow. Her mouth turned dry all at once, tongue tasting of ash. It was easier to water the incident down; to water Ruby down. But she couldn't now, and she felt awful for it. No wonder the girl was a mess.

"She might be a pain in your arse, but that's your job: to look after people who are difficult, people who have been through hell and back. It's what you agreed to when you started this. Just give the girl a bloody break, would you? You don't have to be nice to her. Just stop making life more difficult for her. It's not who you are." Liam glanced at her from head to toe as though weighing her up. "Or, at least, it didn't use to be."

He walked away with those words, boots crunching through gravel as he headed back into the farmhouse to swap shifts with Eric. She was left alone, red-faced and scolded and *hurt*. Because she knew what Liam had meant when he'd said *it didn't use to be*. He meant before the accident. Before she'd been forced to retire. And he used that against her on purpose to make his point.

"*Dick*," she muttered. He knew her too well sometimes. In her efforts to hold everyone at arm's length, she'd almost forgotten that.

With a sigh, Shea made her way inside as well, pulling her phone from the pocket of her leggings and considering it for a moment. There was a sudden, unexpected urge to open her search browser and type in Ruby's name; to see how much of Ruby was exactly what Shea expected, of what news outlets were saying about the accident. But Shea didn't need to be fed false or overexaggerated information, and it felt like a violation, somehow, to go looking for it.

So she didn't. She would make up her own mind about Ruby. And she would at least try to stop being so ruthless and judgemental in the process.

* * *

Ruby slept through the rooster's crows, and she didn't wake until the sun was bleeding obnoxiously through the cracks between her curtains. The clock ticking on the wall said it was almost noon. At least she had finally caught up on some lost sleep.

Before daring to venture out and no doubt come across Shea, Ruby took her time in the shower and, after getting dressed, finally trudged into the kitchen, spine stiff as though readying herself for battle. But Shea wasn't in the house. She was working in the garden, forking through the soil and transporting heaps of it in wheelbarrows.

Ruby sighed her relief and sat, finding a sandwich piled with bacon on the kitchen table. Flint scampered in from the living room and sat obediently in front of Ruby, probably growing used to her feeding him scraps. But Ruby's stomach grumbled and she still felt wobbly from the day before, so she scarfed it down and hoped it hadn't been meant for one of her security team.

And then, after ten minutes of counting the kitchen tiles and wondering how the hell she could spend her day if she wasn't allowed to help out around the farm, she huffed and gave in. Though well-rested, she still felt awful and on edge. She couldn't stay in here all day. She refused to.

So, she risked venturing into the garden; and when Shea didn't look up from where she now crouched while planting something, Ruby hovered over her, blocking out the low sun and leaving Shea in her shadow.

Shea's mud-caked fingers stopped their planting. She lifted her glance slowly, squinting as green eyes, near translucent in the daylight, settled on Ruby's face. Ruby fought to keep her composure. She wouldn't be talked to the way she was last night. She wouldn't let Shea O'Connor decide what she did here day in and day out. She'd had enough of that to last a lifetime.

"Where can I help today?"

Sighing, Shea went back to pressing seeds into the soil and covering them. "In the house."

"Doing what?"

"Didn't we have this conversation last night?" She rose and swiped the dirt from her hands onto her frayed jeans. "You're not working today. You can go and watch *Loose Women* or whatever crap they air on daytime telly these days. If you get bored, there are plenty of books to occupy yourself with."

"Please, Shea." Ruby hadn't meant to beg or sound so weak, but the words escaped her without permission, hanging between them like a wispy, pathetic cloud. "I want to *do* something. I won't go crazy like yesterday."

Shea's cool eyes danced across Ruby again, hesitant. "Have you eaten today?"

"Yes."

"Drank water?"

"Yep."

She chewed on her lip hesitantly and then said, "All right. You can plant some veg for me." Shea handed Ruby a trowel and motioned to a pot of sprouting seeds she'd been midway through planting. "Careful with the roots."

Ruby fought back a pout. It would hardly keep her busy. Still, she was grateful for anything, especially with the crisp autumn sunshine beating down on her, so she sat carefully and began her work.

Clearing her throat, Shea retrieved a large shovel that had been leaning against the rickety fence and continued upturning a mound of earth a few metres away. Ruby tried not to flinch against the harsh sound of the metal being thrust into the clay soil, through hard stones and grainy patches of dirt.

They worked in silence that way, Ruby intentionally taking her time with each plant and smoothing down the moist soil around it. It took twice as long with one hand anyway. She wrinkled her nose as black began to gather in the crescents beneath her fingernails, wondering why

Shea didn't have any gloves. She didn't think it wise to ask.

"Look, I was too harsh on you last night," Shea said finally, slicking back a few golden strands of hair from her face. Her hands left smears of dirt in their wake, peppering her face and leaving something foreign stirring in Ruby's gut.

Attraction? She pushed the thought away before it could touch her. Shea might have been pretty in a rugged, hard-faced sort of way, but that was where it ended. She was rude and sarcastic and looked down on Ruby, and Ruby couldn't let herself see Shea that way.

"Just last night?" Ruby knew she was testing her luck, but... was the woman trying to *apologise*? That didn't sound like something Shea would do.

Shea's features turned sour as she continued digging, her sinewy arms rippling beneath the plaid sleeves of her loose, unbuttoned shirt. Beneath, damp pooled at her chest, darkening the cotton of her camisole and leaving the material to cling to the soft outline of her stomach.

Stop. Ruby tore her gaze away again, back to the plants.

"Forget it," Shea muttered.

"No, please, do go on."

A heavy, irritated sigh followed by the shovel piercing through the soil again. "I didn't know about your boyfriend. That you lost him in the accident."

Ruby's hand stilled, an automatic lump rebuilding itself in her throat. *Boyfriend* sounded wrong. Reductive. Ezra had been so much more than just a *boyfriend*, and Ruby hated Fusion, Mason, for ever making her pretend otherwise. "I don't need your pity."

"Good. You don't have it. I'm just saying... I shouldn't have pushed you so hard."

"Then why did you?" She couldn't look at Shea as she asked. Couldn't do anything but chew on her cheek and pluck blades of grass from the dirt.

"Because—" A sharp intake of breath replaced Shea's next words, and then the clatter of the shovel to the ground and a whispered, "*Shite.*"

Ruby leapt to her feet before she had time to wonder what was wrong. Shea was hunched over, a hand on the base of her back and her face scrunched in pain.

"What's wrong?"

Shea waved a hand dismissively and tried to straighten, wincing again as she did. "Nothing."

"Shea...." Ruby didn't know what to do. Panic ratcheted through her chest, ebbing only when Shea gulped down a deep breath and seemed to ease. Her face was smattered with colour, gleaming with sweat, chest heaving through strained breaths. "Should I get someone? Liam, or —"

"No. No, I'm fine. Just a bad back is all."

But it didn't look like just a bad back. It

looked as though the pain had drained Shea, left her terrified. She gathered a trembling bottom lip between her teeth, tucking her hair behind her ears with fingers just as shaky. Ruby frowned, inching towards her. Even Flint sprinted out of the garden to whirl around her feet.

"You should sit. Take a break."

"Funny. I think I recall a similar conversation yesterday." She smirked, though it didn't quite meet her eyes as she began to wander slowly back into the house. At least she was more obedient than Ruby. "I'll make an early lunch. Let me know when you're done with the veg patch."

Something tugged Ruby forward. She wanted to ask what was really wrong. She wanted to make sure Shea was okay. But that was none of her business, and Ruby had no reason to care for somebody who had been nothing but rude to her since she'd arrived.

Still, she remembered the food Shea had made last night. The way she'd forced her inside just before Ruby reached the point of collapse. And as Ruby settled back into the grass reluctantly, something in her still niggled and pulled her focus on the open back door, the kitchen within.

She ignored it. Shea had made it quite clear she was fine and didn't need Ruby's help. Ruby wouldn't embarrass herself by checking in on her again.

✳ ✳ ✳

Shea was pushing herself too hard with the farm. She didn't want to admit to it, though, not even when the pins and needles began to spark through her legs again. Unlike Ruby, she at least had the good sense to know her limits. She'd taken the rest of the day off, with the exception of feeding the animals, of course. Feeling that familiar jolt in her spine again after so long spent recovering had petrified her. She couldn't go back to before. Couldn't end up destroying something she had worked so hard to rebuild.

The worries plagued her when she tried to sleep that night. Eventually, she gave up, socked feet scuffing across the old floorboards as she crept through the house in search of distraction. A book, maybe. The dead of night was the only time she had the chance to read, anyway. Might as well make the most of it.

When she reached the living room, though, she realised she wasn't the only one awake at one o'clock in the morning. Honey-golden light slipped beneath the door, soft footsteps creaking behind it. Liam or Leona taking a break from their shift, perhaps.

Or perhaps Shea was just very unlucky because when she pushed the door open, it wasn't a guard standing by the window — it was Ruby.

Ruby turned when the door creaked, surprise and then trepidation flickering across her features. She leaned against the piano, and the cover was open. The most it had been touched in years. Across the room, Flint was curled up on the sofa, his snores sounding like one of the pig's grunts. Shea had barely seen the dog at all since Ruby moved in.

"Oh." Ruby shut the cover quickly and wrapped her thin satin robe around her, though she wore her pyjamas beneath. Revealing pyjamas, Shea couldn't help but note, with the plunging camisole top and shorts set, but pyjamas nonetheless. "Sorry. Did I wake you?"

Shea shook her head. "You're all right. I couldn't sleep. Just came for a book." She scoured the bookshelf, plucking up a random clothbound copy of an old classic. Beneath Ruby's scrutiny, she couldn't focus enough to read the title. "Were you going to give us a midnight serenade?"

Ruby's cheeks flushed pink, eyes falling to her bare feet. "No."

"You can use it, you know. I mean, preferably not in the middle of the night, but during the day, it's all yours."

She considered this, fingers dancing across the top of the piano as though tempted. "Can't really play with one hand."

It sounded more like an excuse than the truth, but Shea wouldn't pry, even if a flicker of curiosity did ignite in her gut. It was strange to imagine Ruby sitting on Shea's mother's old stool. She was so... indifferent. Unfazed. She looked at the musical instrument as though it was an acquaintance she didn't have the time to stop for a polite conversation with.

But maybe that was the grief. Maybe Shea had not been judging Ruby fairly at all.

"Well, if you change your mind, it's there. Someone should get some use out of it."

"You don't play?"

Shea snorted. Her mother had tried to teach her back in Ireland and had swiftly moved her into a few sports teams when she realised she hadn't been gifted with the same musical talents. "No. It was my mam's. Couldn't bring myself to get rid of it."

And it was half-eaten by dust now, like everything else in here.

"Oh."

"Anyway...." Shea shook her book and made to leave, but Ruby's voice brought her back.

"He wasn't my boyfriend. Ezra. The one who...."

Ruby seemed to stumble over the unsaid word, and Shea nodded to show she understood. Still, she didn't see why Ruby was telling her. She had done nothing to earn an explanation.

And yet she had a feeling, somehow, that Ruby wanted to give it. She shifted restlessly, eyes glittering, more open than Shea had ever seen them, and Shea wanted to hear the end of it. She wanted to know. She wanted Ruby to carry on.

"Do you fancy a cup of tea?" she asked.

Ruby's tongue slipped past the seam of her lips and then hid again as she considered. "Yeah.

Yeah, that sounds good."

She followed Shea to the kitchen. Shea boiled the kettle wordlessly, reaching on her tiptoes to pull down the mugs. She hadn't thought about how the movement would cause her pyjama shirt to ride up until Ruby said, "Your back. What happened?"

A pang of dread shot through Shea's chest. She set down the mugs and yanked on her hem, turning around to gauge Ruby's reaction. She wasn't wide-eyed or pale or disgusted, though. Not like some people would be when they saw the puckered, scarred flesh of bullet wounds. Instead, her brows were furrowed, features drawn tight with curiosity.

But something clogged Shea's throat and she couldn't tell Ruby. She didn't want to. Reliving it was too hard. The truth of it was too painful. She might have mostly healed from the injury, but it was a weakness she tried every day to hide. It was difficult when it had left her retired and aimless and sometimes in pain.

So, Shea only asked, "Do you like milk in your tea?"

"Right. Sorry." Ruby's features smoothed with understanding. "Just a drop, please."

Shea made the drinks quickly, glad to be able to sit down where she was less exposed, less likely to give Ruby a glimpse of all the broken parts of her. Hands curled around the warm mug, she waited for Ruby to say something. Finish explaining. Finally, she looked questioningly up at Ruby and found her tracing the thick rim of her mug absently.

Grief was written all over her. In her trembling hands and clenched jaw. The lines in her forehead and the downturned dimples of her mouth. How had Shea been able to ignore it before?

She couldn't push Ruby to talk, so she sipped her tea instead, though it was still scalding hot. And then Ruby seemed to deflate in her chair, and without lifting her eyes, she began. "Everyone thought we were together, but we weren't. It felt... cheap and wrong that you called him that earlier."

"I'm sorry."

"No, I'm not blaming you. You couldn't have known. No one did." Ruby paused to sip her tea, steam curling around her features. "They made us pretend."

"Who did?"

"Management." She said the word with such bitterness that it cut through the tension between them. "They thought it made good publicity."

Shea's brows knitted together. She couldn't imagine her personal life being manipulated for the sake of other people. Couldn't imagine having to live a lie.

"I shouldn't have to lie anymore, should I?" Ruby's voice broke at the end of the question. "He's gone now. I don't want his memory to be a lie. I want—" A jagged intake of breath. Shea was holding her own, feeling too raw, too sympathetic for a girl she had never really seen before now. "He wasn't my boyfriend. He was my best friend, and that meant so much more. I just wanted you to know that. I wish everyone knew that."

"You're right." The softness in Shea's voice surprised even her. "You shouldn't have to lie. I'm sorry that you lost him."

She wondered what it said about her when surprise flared in Ruby's teary eyes. What kind of person was Shea if her showing basic empathy and kindness came as a shock to other people?

Ruby sniffed and took another gulp of tea, averting her gaze to the curtain-covered windows. "Thank you."

They sat that way in utter silence, wrapped in the stillness of night, until the last dregs of tea had been drained and the birds began to chirp outside. And then they went back to bed without saying goodnight — yet somehow, it felt as though they had said so much more without it ever leaving their mouths.

Shea had to shake the guilt and sorrow before she rose again the next morning.

CHAPTER FOUR

After ten days of walking around the same hundred acres of grass, and just as many evenings wandering within the same four walls, Ruby had succumbed to cabin fever. While things were no longer as tense as they first had been with Shea, she was still struggling to figure out how to spend her time when she wasn't helping with the animals or vegetable patches.

It made it worse that she was always being watched. Morning, noon, and night there was a security guard somewhere nearby. She couldn't eat lunch without being eyed sternly by Claire. She couldn't even go to the bathroom without Eric lingering behind her and then blushing when she told him she didn't need a chaperone to have a piss. It was something that Ruby had always tolerated before; it came with fame, after all. But it felt slightly more dehumanising here, with no real threat to protect her from — save for a slightly aggressive cow in the next field over who sometimes tried to barge through the fence to chase Shea's livestock.

She was in the middle of the countryside, endless fields and cloudy skies yawning out around her, and yet she still was not free. And she was *bored*.

She *deserved* to be free and not bored. Just for the day. As though the world wanted to confirm it, Ruby kept catching the glimmer of water between the line of trees fringing Shea's property. So when her minders swapped shifts and Shea prepared lunch at midday, Ruby took the opportunity to sneak away from the vegetable patch she was tending to, shooing off Flint when the Labrador tried to follow her.

It wasn't easy sneaking around out in the open. Shea could glance out of the kitchen window at any moment and catch Ruby in the act. But as the grass grew taller and the earth less trampled by hooves and tractors, she dared a look back... to find that nobody was following her.

Ruby was *free*.

She and Ezra had performed this small act of rebellion together all the time. They would slip away from security and Cerys in foreign cities, finding hidden places where they could just be normal people for a while — usually until they were recognised by fans, but still. Doing this now felt like keeping him alive, somehow. Then again, Ezra probably would have hated everything about the farm. A city boy through and through, he'd never been interested in nature. With the amount of manure she'd stepped in recently, Ruby was beginning to understand why.

The earth became uneven beneath her boots

as she traipsed deeper into the copse of trees towards the sparkling water. She worked hard not to trip over loose roots and unpredictable soil, dandelion seeds assaulting her face and tugging a stream of sneezes from her. Maybe she hadn't thought this through. Her jeans were already covered in burrs, and then she had to fight her way through a wall of thorns and branches to emerge from the woods.

But it was worth it.

Tucked within the heart of rustling leaves, birdsong, and towering woods, Ruby found a stillness she had long since forgotten existed. The water that had called her turned out to be a deserted lake. Algae frothed at the surface of the shore, broken only by the subtle rays of sunlight dripping through trees that were already burnished with the golden promise of autumn.

And not a few metres away, a small rowboat was covered with a weathered, moss-eaten tarpaulin.

Ruby sucked in a relieved, burning breath, drinking in the scent of the earth — loamy and fresh from last night's rain. She could feel the stagnancy of the water as though it had poured itself into her chest, and she could hear the faint hum of insects as though they were a song in her veins. It reminded her of summers as a child, feeding the ducks mouldy bread on a humid day, and then sitting down for a picnic with her parents.

Nobody was here to bother her. Nobody had followed. She was completely alone for the first time in years. She could breathe just for a moment. She could—

A twig snapped somewhere close. Ruby whipped around, narrowing her eyes. She expected to find one of Fusion's team waiting to escort her back to the farm, but there was nobody. Nothing. Just her and the woods and the lake, all undisturbed. Ruby almost smiled.

Almost.

She imagined Ezra standing beside her, kicking his scuffed Doc Martens through the silt and gravel as they complained about management or laughed about something their bassist, Max, had come out with while intoxicated the previous night. She imagined Ezra trying to push her into the water, or daring her to pull the tarp from the boat and get in. They'd always managed to find fun together, even when it had felt impossible.

You and me against the world.

A solemn smile twitched at the corners of Ruby's mouth. She closed her eyes as a cool breeze whispered around her, wondering if it was Ezra's way of telling her he was here. It was silly to believe it, but Ruby wanted to; so she did. She pretended, just for a while, that the wind curling around her was him. And then she dragged the tarpaulin off the rowing boat — an awkward manoeuvre with only one good hand — and took it in.

It was chipped and grimy, the once-white paint faded to a murky yellow. Probably not safe to use, but there was nothing in the world that felt safe to Ruby anymore.

"How exactly do you plan to row with one hand?"

The Irish lilt startled Ruby enough that she stumbled away from the boat, a hand on her chest. She turned around, finding Shea standing in the clearing with her arms crossed over her torso. Dirt streaked her face from a morning of labour, her hair tied messily on her head.

And her eyes blazed with anger.

"Jesus Christ," Ruby breathed. "Did you have to sneak up on me?"

"That boat isn't yours," was Shea's only reply, words barbed beneath her usual indifference. "Cover it up and get back to the farm."

Ruby frowned, glancing at the boat again. "Whose is it?"

"None of your business."

Ruby pursed her lips defiantly. She'd had quite enough of obeying Shea's barked commands. She wasn't going to give up her peace to do it again now.

Shea's brows rose when Ruby didn't move, her features pinched into a scowl that seemed more cutting, more personal than usual somehow. As though before, it had been a habit, something that Ruby could brush off easily enough, but now it was aimed at her with purpose.

"I mean it, Bright," Shea said. "They're about to send out a search party up there."

"Well, you found me."

"Somewhere you shouldn't be."

"Whose boat is it?" Curiosity niggled at Ruby now. She searched the boat for some telltale sign of its owner, a name or even initials, but there was nothing. "Is it yours?"

The only response she received was a hissed sigh. Ruby thought for a moment that Shea might haul her back to the farm kicking and screaming, but she remained a marble statue between the trees.

"You don't give up, do you?" Shea questioned finally.

"No."

Shea's throat bobbed as her eyes fell past Ruby to the boat, irises the same deep green as the damp moss. "The boat was my mam's, all right? It's not yours to touch."

By the looks of it, it seemed it wasn't *anyone's* to touch. Ruby's brows furrowed as she scrutinised it again. She couldn't imagine a woman like Shea ever rowing out on the lake in it. "Where is she now? Your mum, I mean."

A muscle danced in Shea's sharp jaw. It was the only sign of discomfort she showed. "Dead."

The word cut between them like an axe — but it didn't sever whatever connected them. Whatever had seemed to connect them since the night Shea had made Ruby tea and Ruby had told her about Ezra. Ruby only felt the invisible rope pull stronger now, tighter, until Ruby was inching forwards without even realising it.

Mine too, she wanted to say. Instead, she opted for: "I'm sorry."

A shrug. And then Shea brushed past Ruby to collect the tarp from the ground. "Do me a favour and tell me next time you fancy a wander."

"I was getting cabin fever up there. They watch me constantly."

"It's their job." Shea's face tightened with severe lines as she straightened the tarp out, cursing frustratedly when it remained creased. "For feck's sake, come on you bloody thing."

Guilt pricked Ruby when she heard the slight quiver in Shea's voice. In uncovering the boat, it seemed she had unleashed shadows, grief, in Shea that Ruby hadn't known existed. She bit her lip and peeled the curling tarp from Shea's hands.

"Can't we use it?" Trepidation left Ruby's voice meek.

Shea stilled, features indecipherable. "What?"

"The boat. Couldn't we use it?"

"You want to go out on the lake in a twelve-year-old rowing boat that's falling apart?"

"Yes," Ruby admitted. "Aren't you sick of the farm? Of working constantly? I'm going to lose the plot if I shovel one more heap of horse poo."

Shea's lips flickered with the ghost of a smile, and Ruby knew it was about as good as she'd ever get with the guarded woman. It was enough. With the small dimples sinking like apostrophes into her chin, it was enough.

"Come on, Shea. Just for a little while?" It had been a long time since Ruby had pleaded for anything. But it was as though she had woken to find everything slightly more real today. She wasn't suffocating in a wave of grief, though that heaviness in her heart remained and probably always would. The ground was sturdier beneath her feet. Noises sounded louder, closer. Colours seemed more vibrant. And it made her want to feel something again. It made her want to do what she would have done with Ezra: break the rules, find peace in an unexpected place, row a beaten boat through a sun-dappled lake when she should have been working with three other pairs of eyes on her.

She didn't expect Shea to cave — and yet Shea wilted, all the same, running a hand across the splintered edge of the boat. "Liam'll have my head if you drown."

Ruby smiled, and it was so unexpected and unpracticed that her cheeks seemed to crack like dry plaster. "That sounds like a 'yes' to me."

❋ ❋ ❋

Siobhan O'Connor would be rolling in her grave if she'd known that a celebrity was currently occupying the boat she had spent years in the old barn working on. Shea had inherited all of her worst traits from her mother and, while she had loved the woman dearly, she could admit that Siobhan had been grumpy and difficult at the best of times.

Shea had to bite down a smile as she imagined it, rowing one oar while Ruby managed the other. The water rippled in soft, fly-infested peaks, smoother — but not clearer — than Shea expected it to be after so many years lying stagnant. In truth, she avoided coming down here when she could. It was too easy to get wrapped up in her grief here. Shea always felt closer to Siobhan here in a way she never had with the farm or the dusty grand piano, the china plates or the old cloth-bound books. Her mother had poured just as much of herself into the boat as she had everything else, and Shea remembered Sundays spent this way together — undisrupted by the outside world. Just the two of them, surrounded by verdant walls that kept everything else out. Other than farmwork, it was the only time they'd really spent together.

Perhaps Shea understood why Ruby had come here. That didn't mean she'd been impressed by the disappearing act earlier.

In front of her, Ruby drank in a long breath and tilted her head to the sun. The light kissed her closed, tired eyes in shifting rays, gilding her dark, wavy strands of hair. And maybe Shea had to force herself to look away as unexpected warmth bloomed within her. Maybe she had to remind herself of who Ruby was, and who Shea was, and what that meant.

She lifted her oar from the water, arms aching and sweat beginning to bead in her hairline. "Happy?"

An unexpected, brittle smile curled across Ruby's heart-shaped lips, and she stopped rowing as well. "Yes."

The wooden bench supporting Shea creaked as she shifted to better soak in the tranquillity around her. She couldn't remember the last time she had ever stopped to notice it, not like this. It should have been impossible with someone else there, and yet it felt easy somehow. Just like it had that night when Shea and Ruby had sat in silence in the kitchen. Perhaps Ruby was a pain in the arse, but there was an understanding between them that felt magnified now — a shared shadow that loomed over them both.

"Did your mother own the farm, too?" Ruby questioned, eyelash-framed lids peeling open again to look at Shea. Her dark irises were molten amber in the light, bleeding into rings of black.

Shea nodded, the only answer she would give. It was rare that she talked about her mother aloud. She wouldn't know how to now, even if she tried. After a messy divorce a decade before her death, her father didn't want to discuss Siobhan with Shea when she called or visited, and nobody else knew her the way Shea did.

"When…." Ruby nibbled her bottom lip hesitantly and then tried again. "When did she die?"

"Are we going to do this?"

"What?" A frown disrupted Ruby's smooth

features.

Shea motioned between them. "Talk like we're friends."

"I suppose not." Ruby sank back, clasping her hands between her legs and sighing. Her mouth tugged down into a pout, and she seemed to hesitate before speaking again. "What's your problem with me, Shea?"

"I don't have a problem," Shea muttered, taken aback by the question.

"You've been nothing but hostile toward me since I got here."

"Yeah, well, don't flatter yourself into thinking you're special. I'm hostile toward everybody. It's in my blood."

"Not with Liam," Ruby pointed out. "You're friends. Sometimes he even makes you laugh."

"I've known Liam a long time."

She studied Shea as though she didn't believe her, though it was the truth. Shea was her mother's daughter. Standoffish was her nature. It had only amplified around Ruby, perhaps because she'd assumed the worst in her. Maybe that was unfair. Maybe Shea should have been more welcoming. But did it matter? They weren't supposed to be friends. This wasn't a holiday for Ruby. It was a necessary precaution. Shea wasn't her friend; she was just the person who offered out her safe house.

"You think I'm spoilt."

"No," Shea countered, though it was only a half-truth. Ruby had been living here for over two weeks now and still wore Gucci-branded boots and fancy jumpers. Rationally, Shea knew that was all superficial, but she couldn't help but feel Ruby looked down on her, on the farmhouse. She knew it was old and bordering on ramshackle, but it was safe and gave Ruby the protection she needed. That should have been enough.

"I didn't grow up with money, you know," Ruby continued. "My parents were in debt before they died, and then my aunt took me in even though she worked night shifts for minimum wage. Everything I have now, I earned — and I did it so that my family would never be in that position again."

Shea supposed that was meant to impress her. It didn't. She had spent her life working hard too, and it had never gotten her anywhere — save for retired at thirty-three and running her mother's farm to the ground. "Okay. Good for you."

Ruby clucked her tongue impatiently. "If you can't even talk to me like I'm a real person, why did you bring me out here?"

"If I'd have known you'd throw a bloody paddy, I wouldn't have!" Shea began rowing again, the paddles slapping the water viciously this time as they inched their way towards the shore.

Like a petulant child, Ruby crossed her arms over her chest, nostrils flaring. "So we're going back to this?"

Jesus Christ. The woman was impossible. Shea had tried to be more understanding. She'd tried to be kinder. She'd taken her out in her mother's bloody boat when she'd asked and made her tea at midnight. "I don't know what you expect from me."

"Not much, Shea," Ruby snarled. "Just a conversation that doesn't end in you tearing into me."

The venom in her voice surprised Shea enough that she stopped paddling. "Why does it matter if we have a fecking conversation or not? We're not here to braid each other's hair and talk about boys. I'm not your friend."

"And you've made that abundantly clear."

Shea blew out an impatient breath. "So go and have a conversation with someone else. I'm sure Liam is available for all of your social needs."

"Nobody else understands!" Ruby's voice wavered and crested, a tidal wave breaking onto the shore and swallowing everything in its path. Shea gulped against it, icy confusion and something else — something she didn't want to acknowledge — pooling in her gut.

Ruby seemed to register her own words and her face paled, hands lifting halfway to her face and then falling back into her lap.

"Understands what?" Shea asked, words low.

Ruby's eyes glittered with tears as they darted away from Shea, to the swaying water. "In the kitchen that night, when I told you about Ezra, I thought maybe you understood. Nobody has listened to me like that since he...." Her swallow was strained and audible. "Since the accident. And then you mentioned your mum."

It was an effort for Shea to remain composed, brows drawn closely and jaw locked with tension. "So we're to bond over our shared grief, are we?"

"No. No, clearly you have no interest in talking about anything other than cows and horses and how spoilt and useless I am."

Shea's fingers clenched around her paddles, knuckles turning white. "I don't owe you anything else."

"I just wanted to know how you manage it." Another crack tore through Ruby's voice. Another bout of pain Shea didn't want to notice bled through. "That's all. I just wanted to know how I'm supposed to carry on."

Shea couldn't help but soften with sympathy, her own heart wrenching in her chest. The woman was shattering in front of her, grief her only friend. And Shea was an arsehole. She knew that. But she had grown too used to pushing people away. Too used to keeping her wounds hidden. The last time she had opened herself up, it nearly destroyed her — more than the injury and more than her mother's death.

"There is no 'how'," Shea murmured finally, the boat rocking them towards the shore on the whisper of Shea's earlier rowing. "You just *do*. You manage it. You carry on. You let it swallow you every day and then you claw yourself out just to wake up the next morning and do it all again. And then one day you notice it's not as difficult to bear, and you don't know why. It just… isn't."

Ruby's lips parted, a tear trickling down her cheek. "Thank you. That's… it's all I wanted to hear. Thank you."

"I don't hate you, Ruby," Shea confessed because she had laid herself bare, let Ruby in, and she couldn't find a way back out. "I just…." She couldn't finish that sentence. Didn't try. "I don't hate you."

Ruby nodded and wiped her cheeks. "Good."

They didn't talk again as the boat crawled back to shore.

CHAPTER FIVE

Ruby woke two days later with a new melody humming through her bones and a jumble of half-formed lyrics echoing in her mind. She tried to ignore it at first. She and Ezra had always written music together and it felt like a betrayal to do it any other way.

But as she mucked out the horses with Shea, a steady and surprisingly easy cadence of conversation falling between them, the song began to tug at her chest and split through her skin, a writhing creature desperate to be set free.

With no other option, she sat at the grand piano after dinner that evening and played.

It was a stilted string of wrong keys at first, made all the worse by the fact Ruby could only use one hand. She tried with the other, but the cast chafed at her knuckles and her fingers didn't have the freedom they longed for. Still, it was something, and it made her feel... lighter, somehow, to let it out. It made her feel closer to Ezra. She imagined him sitting beside her on the bench, pressing down the keys she couldn't reach and humming the lyrics she hadn't yet figured out under his breath.

The first line came easily after that: *You said it was you and me against the world, but now you're gone.*

Ruby made sure to sing it quietly, her voice cracked and alien after weeks of nothing but stifling sobs. She took a deep breath before writing it down in her old, leather-bound notebook, steeling herself against the pain. It wasn't easy to write *about* him instead of *with* him. But she needed it. She needed an outlet for her grief. When she had nothing else, she had music. It was the thing that had brought her and Ezra together — and maybe the thing that tore them apart in the end.

She scrawled down a few more lines, unnamed emotions that had been bubbling away inside her until now. And then she found a tune for the bridge, imagining how it would sound if she had both hands and the band with her.

But she'd never have the band with her again. She didn't even know where Max was now or how she was handling Spencer's and Ezra's deaths. Ruby had seen her only once after the crash, and they'd both been too in shock to say more than a few words to one another.

"You found a way to play then?"

The voice came from above and dragged Ruby from her thoughts. On instinct, she slammed her notebook shut with the pen still caught between the pages and lifted her gaze to find Shea hovering at the door. A gentle smile, a smile that Ruby didn't think she'd ever earn from the farmer, tugged at her mouth, her hair twisted into a damp rope across her shoulder.

Ruby tried to shake off the embarrassment she felt, shuffling away from the piano keys and shrugging. "Not very well, but it's a start."

"Sounded grand enough to me." Shea stepped into the room and collapsed onto the couch, where Flint had curled up with a cushion. "Is it new?"

"Yeah. I doubt it will ever see the light of day, though." Unintended bitterness soured Ruby's words, and she picked at a loose strip of skin on her thumb to avoid Shea's disarming gaze.

"Oh? Why's that?"

"The label rejects any idea that isn't about meaningless shit like partying and sex," she admitted. "That, and... well, I don't really have a band to sing with now, do I?"

"You wouldn't go solo?" It was strange to hear the glimmer of curiosity in Shea's voice. They had been getting on a little better since rowing on the lake, but Ruby always felt out of place in her presence. Shea was steadfast, with her roots thrust firmly in the soil around them. She was strong and hardworking and never gave a hint towards what lay beneath her cool façade. Ruby was the opposite. She was wrapped up in all things superficial, things that she knew Shea looked down upon, and she wasn't strong enough to hide her emotions.

Sometimes, though, it felt as though if Shea just reached out, shared that strength, gripped

Ruby tightly, Ruby might be able to stand a little taller too. It made no sense, but her chest always fluttered with *want* around Shea. She wanted to understand Shea better. She wanted Shea to understand her better. She wanted....

She didn't really know what she wanted, only that it was more than Shea would probably ever be willing to give. So, she closed the fallboard and swivelled on the bench to face Shea, relishing a rare moment where they felt civil, two equals able to have a conversation about something other than how to tend to pigs or how long it took for the chickens to lay their eggs.

"No, I don't think so. Not now. Ezra and I...." Ruby bit her lip, unsure if she'd be saying too much. But they were in the middle of nowhere, with nobody else to hear them. What did it matter if Ruby told Shea? "We wanted to get out. Once my contract finishes, I'm done. I'd imagine that now I don't have a band, it will be sooner rather than later."

Shea's overlapping front teeth pressed against her bottom lip. "How come? Is being a pop star not all it's cracked up to be?"

Ruby only snorted. She wasn't a pop star. She wasn't much of anything anymore. She might have been bored witless, watched like a hawk, and lost in grief here, but at least she was just Ruby. At least she didn't have a million people telling her where to go and what to do, what to say and how to say it. The more time she spent in the dirt with Shea, the less she wanted to face reality again. It was easy to forget that the flashing lights of a dozen cameras and tabloid headlines slating her with their lies even existed beyond the hills and lakes and trees.

"It's not as easy as it looks," Ruby admitted. And then, cautiously, "What about you?"

"I can't sing."

"Ha," Ruby deadpanned at the less than subtle attempt to evade the question. "I mean what grand plans do you have for the future? Will you stay here on the farm forever?"

"If the alternative is an office job, yes." Absently, Shea brushed her fingers through Flint's fur. It was strange seeing her this way: rosy-cheeked from the shower, dressed in a casual, hole-infested jumper and leggings. Striped socks on her feet instead of muddy Wellies. At ease, comfortable, *still*. Ruby didn't think she had ever seen Shea so still. She was always working, always moving.

"Then your retirement… it's permanent?"

A mirthless smirk. "Yes, it's permanent."

Ruby could only dare whisper, "What happened?"

She didn't expect a reply. Not when Shea's eyes fogged to the same colour as the murky lake they'd rowed on a few days ago. But then Shea blinked, chest rising and neck rippling with a tight breath. "You saw what happened."

The scars on her lower back. But they didn't answer anything. Ruby hadn't had a chance to find any clues in the rough patches of raised white tissue peeking out below her shirt before Shea had turned and hidden them. She only knew that anything able to tear through a woman as powerful as Shea must have been traumatising indeed.

"Was it some sort of accident?"

Another flicker of twisted amusement crossed Shea's face. "No, it was very much on purpose. Though they weren't aiming for me."

Somebody had done it to her. Anger flared unexpectedly through Ruby at that. It was one thing to have something taken from her in an accident, as the one Ruby survived had, but another completely to have harm inflicted on her, have her career robbed because of it. "You were on duty?"

"Yep." Shea nodded as though it meant nothing. "An eyewitness involved with a bad group of people."

"And you...." Ruby's palms gathered with sweat as she tried to picture it: the scars as fresh wounds, Shea bleeding out on the floor, uniformed like Liam and just trying to keep whoever it was safe. "You tried to protect them and ended up in the crossfire?"

Shea's features solidified back to rough stone, and Ruby knew she'd pried too much, pushed too far. "Do you want any supper?" Shea asked, disregarding the question completely.

"No." Rejection bit through Ruby as she shook her head, and then disappointment flooded her when Shea stood and made to leave. "No, thank you."

Ruby waited on the piano stool for Shea to come back. She waited longer than she would have liked to admit, the clock ticking on the mantel behind her, and Flint snoring on the couch the only indication that any time had passed at all.

But Shea didn't return, and, music forgotten, Ruby was left to wonder and imagine her own stories, her own truth, in Shea's absence.

CHAPTER SIX

"My parents used to take me horse riding as a child."

Ruby's confession broke through the quiet of the stable.

Shea arched an eyebrow as she brushed through her favourite horse's chestnut-brown mane, unsure what she had done to earn such candidness from Ruby after the conversation Shea had gracelessly shut down last night. Things were strange between them these days. Too easy. Stranger still was that Shea didn't mind it. In fact, Ruby wasn't terrible company at all.

"Were you any good?" Shea asked.

Ruby kept her eyes focused on Gideon the grey horse she was grooming beside Shea. "I don't know. I was a little too young, I think. I loved it though."

Shea could sense that. She often found Ruby in the stable during the day, even when she'd finished cleaning and feeding the horses. The horses seemed to like her just as much as Ruby liked them, and as though to prove it, Gideon nudged his head against her hand lovingly. Shea tried not to notice the small smile Ruby gave in response, though it made something in her chest pang.

"Why did you stop?"

"Couldn't afford it." Ruby shrugged nonchalantly, but Shea could feel the weight of everything she didn't say. How much she had cared. "And then my parents died and my aunt struggled with money, too, so I just never got the chance to go back."

Shea's hand stilled against Maple's lean torso. If she had gotten through grief before, why had she been so hellbent on asking Shea for help? "I'm sorry."

"What about you? Do you ever ride them?"

A twinge shot through Shea's spine at the very idea. "Can't. It's no good for my back. I used to though." And she missed it. Just to sit a little bit higher, feel Maple's leather reins slide against her palms, hear her hooves trotting through long blades of grass as they rode freely through the fields.

An idea formed then, one that left Shea dropping the brush to retrieve an old saddle from its hook. She couldn't ride anymore, but Ruby could. "You fancy it?"

"Oh!" Ruby glanced warily at the saddle and then Maple, who was the tallest — but tamest — of all of Shea's horses. "I don't know. It's been a long time."

"I'll keep hold of the reins." Shea's cheeks flamed with the realisation that she was *too* willing. A few days ago, she hadn't been able to think of anything worse than spending more time than necessary with Ruby. Now she was trying to *convince* her to? "You don't have to. It's nearly time for dinner anyway and—"

"I'd like to," Ruby amended quickly, brushing down her hands and taking hold of the saddle to examine it. "Are you sure?"

"Are *you* sure?" A smirk played on Shea's lips — a challenge. For some unknown reason, her heart had sped up in her chest, a warmth bleeding through her veins and, God, she wanted this. If she couldn't ride Maple anymore, somebody else should at least get to. Somebody who cared for the horses as much as Ruby did.

Ruby wrinkled her nose, eyes shifting to the watery-grey light outside. "Eric and Claire aren't going to follow us around, are they?"

"Nah. I'll bribe them to stay put with my cauliflower cheese."

It was the first time Shea had ever seen Ruby's real, unbridled smile, her white teeth flashing like pearls and her freckled cheeks swelling. Her dark eyes sparkled in the stables' shadows. "All right," she said. "Deal."

❉ ❉ ❉

Horse riding was even better than Ruby remembered. The crisp, early-autumn breeze whipping through her hair, the ground smaller, the sky closer. In a world of uncertainty, the rhythmic sway of Maple's steps were something she could rely on — even if she did feel wobbly riding one-handed — and Shea made sure of it by guiding them both by a lead rope beside them.

They travelled slowly across Shea's land, stopping when they reached the farthest fence. Beyond them, the dark clouds were breaking to make way for a rosy sunset, so bright it burned Ruby's eyes. She couldn't remember the last time she had felt so at peace. So safe.

"It's colder than I thought." Indeed, Shea's nose had reddened as though somebody had pinched it. "Do you want to eat back at the house?"

"No." It was barely more than a whisper. "I want to stay here for a while."

"Alfresco it is." Shea tied Maple's reins to the fence post before offering a hand.

Ruby took it, surprised to find it warm, though not soft. Shea's palms were etched with calluses and blisters and, somehow, Ruby preferred them that way. She liked feeling the roughness brush against her own skin, liked the way her whole body seemed to prickle with heat as she dropped down from the horse. Shea didn't let go, not until both feet were planted firmly in the soil — and even then, they seemed to stop in front of one another just for a moment, exploring this sudden moment of contact.

And then Shea dragged her gaze and touch away, and Ruby cleared her throat and braced herself against the fence beside Maple, her hands knotting in the mare's dark mane. "God. I can't remember the last time I watched the sunset."

She could, but she realised the fact only after she'd said it. It had been in Italy with Ezra, just before they'd gone on stage at San Siro stadium as the support group for a popular singer-songwriter. The screaming audience and spotlights had been the only part of Milan they'd gotten to see. *We'll come back*, Ezra had said when Ruby had complained. *When we're not touring, we'll come back and spend the summer sightseeing like proper tourists*.

Ruby shook his voice away, focusing instead on the splinters of the fence clawing through the holes of her jumper and the way her boots sank into the damp soil.

"It's beautiful tonight." Shea's voice was low and smooth as melted butter. It was becoming one of the reasons why Ruby could make it through her day: to hear Shea talking to her without biting out insults. She could still be demanding when she told Ruby what chores needed doing on the farm, but Ruby found herself liking that gruff seriousness now. She even liked never knowing which version of Shea she would get.

She was starting to like Shea.

A warm Tupperware box was handed to Ruby a moment later, and then a fork was rooted out from Shea's backpack. "Hope you like cauliflower cheese."

"I do." Ruby peeled off the condensation-speckled lid and closed her eyes against the freed fragrant steam. "My mum used to make this for me all the time. I went through a phase where I refused to eat anything else."

"I can't imagine the havoc it must have wreaked on your digestive system," Shea jested, digging into her own portion. They ate in silence for a few moments, the light passing slowly over their faces, and then Shea asked, "What happened to your parents?"

"A fire." She fought to keep her voice steady, though talking about it never seemed to get any easier. "I was on a school trip at the time so I didn't find out until I got back, but... our apartment building caught fire. We lived on the eleventh floor. They couldn't get out in time."

"Jesus." Shea winced and shifted. "That's awful. I'm sorry, Ruby."

For an excuse to avoid replying, Ruby shoved another piece of cauliflower into her mouth. And then she remembered the boat on the lake. Shea talking about her mother — or not talking. She hadn't wanted to then, but... things had changed. Ruby had shared enough about herself. She was beginning to suspect that Shea was just the sort of woman you had to keep trying with if you wanted to *really* know her. A matryoshka doll with infinite figures hiding within, all different sizes and faces.

And Ruby wanted to know every one of them.

"What about *your* mum?"

There. It was out now. Shea could either answer it or go back to being prickly and annoyed.

She did neither of those things at first, instead releasing a ragged sigh and stabbing through her food distractedly. "Cancer," she mumbled finally.

"It must have been really hard. I'm sorry." Ruby's hand dared to crawl across the fence, closer to Shea's. When Shea didn't recoil, she shuffled her feet closer too, until their elbows almost touched. "What about your dad?"

"He's back in Ireland." Shea offered the ghost of a grim smile and abandoned her meal on the post. Her fingers curled around the fence's top slat, just inches from Ruby's. It would only take a tiny movement for their fingers to brush, and Ruby was tempted to feel those roughened hands in hers again. "Bloody useless, he is. Anyway." She blinked away the glossiness in her eyes, all traces of vulnerability gone in an instant. "Finish your tea."

"Yes, ma'am," Ruby obeyed, but she could barely chew her food for the wings beating in her stomach. The sunset, the moment, Shea... Ruby could feel it slipping through her fingers as quickly as it had come, and she didn't want it to. She wanted to keep it. Wanted to always have the earthy smell of the farm in her nostrils and Shea's delicate voice in her ears. She wanted *more*, because, somehow, no amount of Shea ever felt enough.

She must have shivered because Shea tutted and unzipped her fleece jacket before draping it carefully across Ruby's shoulders. The scent of hay and rain and lemony detergent clung to it, and Ruby let herself be wrapped in it just for a moment. "Aren't you cold?"

"Nah." It was a lie. Ruby could see Shea's breath clouding in front of her.

"Thank you." Finishing the last few bites of cauliflower cheese, Ruby set down her Tupperware and slid her good arm into the sleeve. She didn't have the energy to wrestle her cast into the other. "You know, you're not as mean as you used to be."

"*Pfft*," Shea puffed out. "I was *never* mean."

"You were a *little* bit mean." Ruby kept her tone light, teasing, wondering when she had last been able to bring herself to even talk like this without grief anchoring her somewhere low and unreachable.

"Well, *you* were a little bit annoying."

"You mean I'm not anymore?"

Shea cast her a sidelong glance, lips curling with suppressed amusement. "Don't push your luck, love."

It was answer enough.

Ruby couldn't help herself when she moved closer still, glimpsing the way the sunset sliced Shea's face with shadows and buttery golds, the way her green eyes flashed brighter. She might have been rugged and soil-smeared and too focused on the farm to care about much else, but beauty still lingered on her features. Subtle if you didn't look closely enough.

But Ruby did look closely. She had been look-ing closely for days, weeks, now.

"I like it when we're like this," she found it in her to admit. It came out cracked and uncertain. A whisper lost to the wind.

But she knew Shea heard by the way she tensed. A blonde strand of hair whipped across her face in the icy breeze, and Ruby had to fight not to reach out and tuck it away. They were so close. Any moment, she knew Shea would pull away, or maybe it would be Ruby who lost her courage, and they would go back to the house and lose this shared magnetic pull that felt tangible between them now.

Sure enough, Shea pushed off the fence and cleared her throat. "We should get back. Liam will start his shift soon, and he won't be best impressed to find out I've whisked you away on a horse."

Forget Liam, Ruby wanted to say. *Forget all of that. Let it be just us, here, now, where things don't hurt so much and I can breathe and you can laugh with me like maybe you like me.*

But Ruby couldn't say those things. She could only nod her head and help Shea pack away their Tupperware before Maple took her home again.

❉ ❉ ❉

Clutching two steaming mugs of tea, Shea turned from the kettle to find that Ruby had located the generous tower of red wine stowed away in the pantry.

So it was going to be *that* sort of night.

"I don't mean to be rude, but I think you have a problem," Ruby said, craning her neck to glimpse the stacked shelves of unlabelled green bottles.

"If I had a problem, they'd all be gone by now," Shea pointed out, setting the mugs down on the kitchen table. "Are you quite done snooping through my house?"

"*Our* house." Ruby threw a smirk over her shoulder before grabbing the bottle closest. "Can we?"

With a sigh, Shea motioned for Ruby to help herself, collapsing onto a chair and then wincing when it pinched her tailbone. She still hadn't recovered completely from all of the pressure she'd put on it recently; a rude awakening to the fact that she needed to take better care of herself. Wine probably wouldn't help, but it had been a while since she'd helped herself to the collection.

"Corkscrew?" Ruby's lips were still pale from the cold, cheeks still pink, eyes still glossy, and Shea had to force her eyes away before she started admiring her again. Of course, she *was* pretty and perhaps not *such* bad company. Everyone with money had those qualities, mostly because they could afford to buy them. And if Shea had felt an inexplicable coil of heat when their hands had brushed outside, well... it was just the effects of a good sunset and sharing things that were better left buried.

That's what she told herself, anyway. It wasn't true, of course. When Ruby had looked at her, it felt as though those damn inky eyes could burrow through her skin, to the shadows Shea locked beneath. Nobody had ever been able to do that before. Keeping people out was the thing she was best at.

And yet Ruby *saw* her. Ruby *understood*. Because Ruby had lost people too.

"Top drawer." Shea pulled herself from her thoughts, cursing her own idiocy. Ruby was younger than her. And a celebrity. And grieving. Whatever Shea imagined drifting like a feather between them, never quite touching the ground, was just that: an imagining, something without impact. Shea would ignore it until it fell. And then maybe she would trample on it for good measure.

Ruby retrieved the corkscrew and then shifted sheepishly on her feet. "All right. I have a confession to make."

Shea glanced at Ruby's uncertain hands, the one in the cast cradling the wine in the crook of her elbow and the other fidgeting with the screw, and hazarded a guess: "You don't know how to use a corkscrew."

"No." Ruby's lips curled with a self-deprecating smile. "I don't know how to use a corkscrew."

"Come here." Rising back to her feet, Shea huffed and took the bottle of wine. "I suppose you have assistants and servants and whatnot to do these things at home."

"No, I just don't often drink wine."

Shea found that hard to believe. Then again, if Ruby was anything like most young celebrities, she probably got by on vodka and the less-legal substances they sold at parties. "Well, I'm going to teach you. It's a vital life skill."

"Is it?" A lopsided smile. It soon fell when Shea curled her hands around Ruby's, realising what she had done only when soft warm skin brushed her work-hardened palms.

Shea faltered, swallowing against the ashy dryness in her mouth. There was no taking it back. Instead of trying, she played it off, humming in answer to Ruby's question as she adjusted the wings of the corkscrew and buried the spiral into the cork. "It's not that difficult. Just twist."

Their hands twisted the screw together, tendons rippling beneath the fine skin of their wrists: Shea's pale and blue-veined, Ruby's golden and inked with a detailed crescent moon. When the bottle slipped between, Shea clutched it and let Ruby finish the cork off until it finally popped free.

"Look at that." Ruby grinned as though she'd just won a gold medal in an Olympic sport. "I did it."

Shea rolled her eyes and pretended not to find her pride endearing, retrieving two glasses from the cupboard. "Congrats."

The glasses clattered as she placed them

down, and Ruby wasted no time in pouring the glugging red wine — a little too generously. She didn't stop until both were full to the brim.

"Why do you have so much wine, anyway?"

Shea sat and Ruby took the chair opposite, gulping enough of her wine that her expression soured against the sweet taste. She'd regret it in the morning. Siobhan O'Connor was nothing if not fond of strong drink, and she had made sure to show it in her wine ventures.

"My mam used to make her own. Wanted a vineyard like we lived in Italy or something, not the bloody north of England."

Ruby snorted. "Well, it worked."

"Because she ended up cheating and buying three-hundred punnets of grapes shipped over from Spain."

"She sounds like quite a woman."

Shea couldn't help but smile softly as she glanced around the kitchen. Siobhan's kitchen. Shea didn't dare to touch half of it, as though Siobhan might return tomorrow. If she did, Shea wanted it to be just as she'd left it.

But she wasn't coming back. Shea would have to accept that eventually. Have to find her own way around the farm instead of the relentless day-in, day-out grind her mother had taught her. "She was… something. Stubborn lady. Could have found something to argue about alone in an empty room."

"If she's anything like you, I can imagine

89

it." Ruby leaned forwards on her elbows. She was still wrapped in Shea's fleece. Though Ruby was both curvier and taller than Shea, it seemed to drown her, the cuff of the sleeve falling across her knuckles while the other dangled off her shoulder without purpose. "I wish I could be more like that."

"What? Impossible to tolerate?" It was only half a joke. Shea knew just how much razor-sharp abrasiveness she had inherited from her mother. *O'Connors don't pussyfoot about*, Siobhan had told her once when Shea had been trying to figure out how to talk to her dad after the divorce. *We say what needs to be said and do what needs to be done. Plain and simple. No more bloody whining.*

"No." Ruby rolled her eyes, fingers tapping a silent beat against the table. "I wish… I wish I could stand up for myself more. Be stronger."

Shea frowned, surprised. Ruby had seemed plenty strong to Shea. She answered back most of Shea's remarks with her voice a roaring fire. "How'd you mean?"

A sigh and then a shuffle, as though Ruby didn't know whether to elaborate. Her throat bobbed, and she downed the rest of her drink in one. Tomorrow's headache was now a guarantee. "I… I don't know."

No. Siobhan definitely would not have liked Ruby, not when Ruby was mincing her words. But Shea was not her mother, and she had the decency not to pry — instead twirling the glass's stem between her hands with little regard for the droplets of wine it left on the table.

Ruby kept going, though. Her mind made up, she pursed her lips and straightened. "It's management."

"Management?"

She nodded. "Fusion Management, the company I work with. They treated the band like automatons. Made us work twenty-three-hour days without breaks. Barely even had time to eat." She lowered her gaze, thick lashes catching the dim light from above. "I... I collapsed on stage once. Had to get checked by a paramedic halfway through the show. Exhaustion and low iron, they said. They still made me go back on. It wasn't livable, Shea. It was breaking us."

Anger blazed to life within Shea as she imagined it, leaving a thundering in her ears. She flexed her fingers to keep from showing it. "Jesus."

"We couldn't get out." Ruby's voice fell quieter, wavering, and Shea leaned closer just to hear her. She could reach for Ruby's hand so easily if she wanted to. She *did* want to. But she couldn't cross that line. "We were contracted for five years, and they were practically unbreakable. I know how it sounds. Poor, rich, little musicians who couldn't handle the fame. But it was awful. It drained the joy out of music, and I didn't see half of the money we earned anyway. It was all locked away. I sometimes wished that all the gigs I did would ruin my vocal cords so that it would finally stop. How terrible is that?"

"It's not terrible," Shea muttered delicately, thinking of herself on the farm. Thinking of how every day, it was an effort to get out of bed, an effort to slog her way through shit and mud and hay, just to wake up the next day and do it all over again. She loved the animals, and the farm would always be home, but could she spend the rest of her life like this? Her back was already pleading for her to stop as it was, and she was too young to destroy her body for good. "Nothing is worth ruining yourself over. Nothing."

"Ezra thought the same." Ruby's voice wobbled on his name, and sympathy flooded in Shea. She inched closer, just to let Ruby know she was there. "He wanted to come clean about it all. Tell the press about all the mistreatment. I feel like I owe it to him to do it, but I'm scared, Shea. I could lose everything, and I don't know who I am if I'm not 'Ruby Bright.'"

Shea couldn't fight it anymore. She shifted her chair closer, the wooden legs chafing against the tiles, and then placed her hand on top of Ruby's. Ruby's eyes flickered up, lips parting as though she couldn't quite comprehend it.

"You know, I've had Ruby Bright strutting around my farm for a good few weeks now, and I happen to think she's not so bad even without a microphone and a stage," Shea whispered. "You've survived worse things than losing your fame and fortune. But you should only do it if it's what *you* want, not just because you think Ezra would want it."

Tears sparkled in Ruby's eyes. As she bowed her head, a dark tendril of hair fell across her face. Shea couldn't help but brush it away, and the tear on her cheek with it too. She needed to see Ruby. And she needed Ruby to see her. More than she needed to be cautious. More than she needed to ignore the pounding in her heart or deny the fluttering, serrated-edged wings in her stomach. She felt awful for making Ruby work so hard when she first arrived. For not considering what she might have been through. For assuming the worst. Now, she could barely find a bad thing about her.

"I don't know what will happen when I leave this place." Ruby's chin wobbled, her gaze locking onto Shea's. "I don't think I *want* to leave. I think... I think I *like* it here. With you."

"Well, the farm isn't going anywhere." And then, because Shea had forgotten herself in learning about Ruby: "And neither am I."

Their noses brushed. Shea hadn't even realised they were sitting that closely until she felt it. She could smell the syrupy-sweet wine on Ruby's breath now, and the sharp dewiness of the cool evening they'd bathed in before coming inside. She could feel Ruby's flyaway hairs tickling her cheeks and see the delicate lines of years-long battles etched into her forehead. A beauty spot an inch from her Cupid's bow. A keyhole-shaped scar at the side of her temple.

Her breath hitching as Ruby closed the distance between them.

It was wrong. Shea knew it was wrong. But when Ruby's silken lips pressed against Shea's chapped ones, she couldn't think of pushing her away. Her bones turned to jelly, her heart flatlined, and her mind emptied of anything but Ruby and her salt-laced, wine-sweet kisses.

And then a creak somewhere close — but not from either of them. Shea pulled away still gasping for air, her body as tensed and tingling as a lightning bolt, and searched for the source of the noise. She expected Flint.

It wasn't Flint.

Claire emerged from the corridor, hovering gingerly in the threshold. "Sorry. The plumbing in the security office is broken and Liam said you wouldn't mind if I had one here instead."

"Yeah." Shea hopped up from her chair as though it had grown thorns, tucking her hair behind her ear and not daring to look at Ruby. Her fingers were trembling. Everything was trembling. "No worries. I'll take a look at the plumbing tomorrow for you."

"Cheers," Claire thanked, pale eyes passing between Shea and Ruby. Shea tried not to squirm. She didn't know Claire well. She worked for Ruby's security team, not the Metropolitan Police like Liam. Shea couldn't even begin to imagine how unprofessional it looked — because it bloody well was.

A fury made only for herself flooded Shea

then, and she cleared her throat. "I'm off to bed, anyway."

"Shea." Ruby's voice was nothing more than a faint plea, and Shea tried her best to tune it out as she brushed past Claire to walk away.

She still felt the ghost of Ruby's lips on hers when she closed her bedroom door.

CHAPTER SEVEN

Shea was roused from sleep by a jostling at her shoulder and warm hands pressing into her bicep. A light sleeper, it wasn't in her to wake slowly. She sprang up immediately, flicking on the lamp on her bedside table and almost knocking it to the floor in the process.

"Christ on a bike, Liam," she breathed when she found familiar warm features peering back at her, half-concealed by shadows and darkened by unshaven scruff around his chin. And then she noticed his wide eyes and pursed lips, his troubled expression, and dread trickled like ice in her gut. She glanced at the time on her phone. Three-thirty a.m. There was never a pleasant reason to be woken at this hour. "What? What's wrong?"

"It's better that you come and see for yourself."

The trickle of dread turned into a suffocating deluge. "Ruby? Is she—"

"She's fine. She's still asleep," Liam assured before Shea could even voice the worries aloud. That at least set her more at ease, her fingers rising midway to her lips as she remembered what they had done last night. How they had fallen into one another, forgetting for a moment who they were. Shea had fallen asleep still thinking of that kiss.

She followed Liam into the kitchen, squinting against the transition into brighter light. Eric and Claire stood around the dining table, faces bracketed by wrinkles just as taut as Liam's. Something was very wrong.

"What is it?" Shea repeated, scraping her hair back impatiently. It had fallen out of her ponytail during the night and now hung messily at the nape of her neck.

Gravely, Eric slid something across the table. A piece of paper. Shea snatched it, scanning the words printed in bold-face type.

You can't hide.

"We're afraid Miss Bright's security has been compromised here," Eric began, tenting his fingers with icy calmness. "We don't know how. We don't know who. The security cameras didn't pick up whoever it was, and we've been on duty all night."

Shea gulped down the acid threatening to rise in her throat, placing the note facedown so she wouldn't have to look at it. She knew what it was without having to ask. A threat. Ruby's stalker. "Where did you find it?"

"Pushed through the letterbox," Liam said quietly. "That's not all." He paced over to the back door, the handle giving easily against his hands, and let the cool morning air slip into the kitchen. When he stepped aside, panic shot through Shea, from the tip of her toes to the crown of her head. Sharp and burning and metallic-tasting. She stepped outside wordlessly, Liam's footsteps following behind her only comfort.

Her yard — it was a carnage of feathers and carcasses. The chickens had been released from their coop, most of them lifeless now in the grass. A few of them still wandered around, pecking at the earth as though nothing was amiss.

"We thought a fox had gotten them at first," Liam explained, voice soft as Shea tried to keep calm. It took everything in her, each muscle solid as stone as she clenched her fists. Her fingernails bit into her palms, but she barely noticed the sting. Barely noticed anything but the bleak landscape littered with her dead poultry. "But there's no blood. No bite marks. Their necks must have been broken. And then we found the note."

"*How*?" was all that Shea could stutter out.

"I don't know. I really don't." Liam scratched at the bristle smattering his jaw, at a loss. "They must have been watching us for hours to know when we were circling to the other side of the house. I swear to God, Shea, I left Leona for five minutes for a bathroom break and a coffee, and then she called me back out to… this."

"Didn't Claire notice anything on the security cameras?" Shea's voice was numb, hollow. She turned away, nausea roiling in her gut. She couldn't look at it anymore.

"Whoever it was knew our blind spots. This isn't just some crazed fan, Shea. This person knows what they're doing."

"So why stop with the bloody chickens?" Anger, then. Anger, and then more nothing. More emptiness. It all came in unpredictable bursts so that Shea didn't know which to expect to feel next and didn't know who she would be in five seconds' time. "Ruby is sleeping in the house. They could have gotten her if they wanted her."

"People like this like to play games. You *know* that. They're waiting for the right moment. They're breaking her down first, letting us know they're smarter than us."

Shea did know that. She had come across plenty of sick people before — people who enjoyed the chase, especially when their target was being protected. But no matter how long she'd worked in and around this field, she would never truly understand the mentality it took to terrorise and ruin.

And it felt worse, somehow, than anything Shea had faced before. This was Ruby. Ruby, who was grieving. Ruby, who she had kissed last night. Ruby, who still slept obliviously in the next room.

As though sensing Shea's shift in concern, Liam said, "We're going to have to relocate her. Leona has been arranging alternative accommodation. We'll leave as soon as she's ready."

"You checked on her? They didn't get in the house?"

"I checked. She's fine."

It would have to be enough. Shea would have to ignore anything but the relief. She would have to ignore the anger, the fear, the disappointment. Ruby was leaving. Ruby was leaving because she was in danger, and Shea's house, Shea.... They weren't enough to protect her anymore.

"You should get the police down, too," Liam continued. "See if they can find anything we couldn't."

"Yeah." She sucked in a deep breath and massaged her temples. She would do that, but not before she'd looked over everything herself. She didn't trust the police. She couldn't even trust the bloody security team here. Maybe it wasn't fair, but she blamed them. *Somebody* should have seen *something*.

Liam's hand found Shea's shoulder and squeezed gently. "Will you be okay here on your own?"

"I can handle myself."

It didn't sound like a lie, but it felt like one. Her safe house had been infiltrated. A place that had been a sanctuary for so many, for so long, had been tarnished. Shea wouldn't be able to take in anybody here anymore. The farm would just be a farm now — if the person who had done this didn't come back to finish what they'd started. The feeling of this ending felt as though layers of skin were being peeled off her bit by bit, leaving her raw and wrong and vulnerable.

"Shea?"

The voice came from behind, from the back door. Shea opened her eyes — she hadn't even realised they were closed — and found Ruby standing on the threshold, Flint beside her and her gown wrapped tightly across her torso. Her hooded eyelids were bleary with sleep, her hair knotted and unkempt as it spilt down her back.

It hurt to look at her, so Shea looked away.

"What happened?"

"Go back inside, Ruby," Shea pleaded through gritted teeth, stepping forward to usher her back.

But Ruby was too damn stubborn, and Shea had expected nothing less. She peered over Shea's shoulder, her slippered feet rising to their tiptoes to gauge the fresh graveyard.

A mangled gasp caught in Ruby's throat. Shea used the distraction to nudge her in without a fight, and Liam closed the door behind them.

"What happened?" Ruby repeated.

"Ruby—" Liam began, but Ruby wasn't asking him. Her gaze remained set on Shea.

"*Shea*. What happened?"

Damn her. Damn her for making Shea be the one to have to say it, to break the news. As though she wasn't concerned enough for Ruby. As though the thought of her in any sort of danger wasn't enough to make frayed, knotted ribbons of Shea's bruised heart. It wasn't even her job. She wasn't supposed to be so affected. But it was Ruby, and it was *her* farm, and it was all falling apart because she'd been stupid enough to kiss her last night. That must have been it. The bloody kiss had cursed them all. Somebody had sensed that brief flicker of hope and happiness Shea had felt and righted it before it stayed.

"They found you," Shea informed her finally, shoving the note over to Ruby. It was up to Ruby if she read it. No matter how much Shea wanted to protect her, she would never shelter her from the truth. Ruby was strong enough to see it.

Still, Ruby's hands trembled as she skimmed over the note with her pointer finger, lips parting and face paling when she'd finished. "How did they find me?"

"We don't know," Claire admitted. "What we do know is that it isn't safe for you here anymore, Miss Bright. We're arranging alternative accommodation, somewhere more secure. It's best to get ready; go pack your things."

Ruby's throat bobbed, but she nodded all the same, eyes still searching Shea. Shea kept her guard up, kept her features neutral. She wouldn't show Ruby that this hurt her. It was always going to end. Ruby was always going to leave. She wasn't safe here, and Shea couldn't be selfish enough to have it any other way.

"I'll help you," she offered. It would be the last moments they had together.

Leona returned from the corridor with her phone still clutched in her hand. "We've got a place somewhere in Dorset. We should get going as soon as possible."

"Give me half an hour," Ruby mumbled,

brushing past Leona. Shea followed her into the bedroom, and Flint trailed at her ankles as though guarding her too. She shut the door on the hushed voices floating from the kitchen, watching numbly as Ruby pulled out a suitcase and began piling in clothes from the wardrobe falling apart in the corner.

"What will *you* do?" Ruby's question wavered with uncertainty, but she didn't look up at Shea, not even when Shea pushed her aside to finish packing for her. If Ruby kept piling it in willy nilly, the case wouldn't be able to shut.

"I'll stay."

"But it isn't safe."

"They're not after me, love," Shea whispered. "I still have a life here. Things that need to be done. It might not be a safe house anymore, but it's still a farm."

"I'm sorry," Ruby said after a few moments of nothing. "I'm sorry I led them here. I'm sorry for what they did."

Shea sniffed, every part of her screaming to stop packing, to look at Ruby, to cup her cheeks in her hands and kiss away the fear and the guilt and the pain the way she had last night. But she didn't. She kept going. Always kept going. "That's not your fault. Don't apologise for that."

"Shea...."

Shea ignored her, rolling socks into the inner pockets and clipping the fastener over the ridiculously tall pile of clothes.

"Shea," Ruby repeated. "I wish you would look at me."

Huffing, Shea straightened and mustered the strength to turn her gaze to Ruby. Ruby's eyes were glossy, eyelashes damp, but it was the only sign of vulnerability Shea could find. She'd faced worse things than this. Shea reminded herself of that.

"We never got time to talk about last night," Ruby said.

Shea couldn't talk about last night. Not now. She went back to the suitcase instead, closing it and zipping it up, wishing with the noise it left that she could zip herself up that easily. Keep herself closed and safe. Ruby too.

"*Shea*," Ruby begged, her hand staunching Shea's movements as it covered hers. "*Please*. Do you always have to be so bloody stoic? Can't you just be here with me for a minute?"

No. No, because if Shea was here with Ruby, she would have to let the pain in, and she couldn't do that. Not now. Letting herself care had been the first in a long line of mistakes she'd made in the last few weeks. Letting herself kiss Ruby would be the last. "There isn't time."

"There *is* time. There must be *something* you want to say to me before I go."

"Like what?"

Ruby stumbled, slapping her arms out dramatically. "I don't know, that you'll miss me? That you hope I'll be okay? That you'll find me when this is all over?"

"Find you for what?" Shea's brows furrowed. She counted the seconds ticking away on her mother's old clock to keep her composure. It hung above the bedroom door, patterned with pigs and chickens. A stark reminder Shea didn't need.

One.

Two.

Three.

Don't show her.

Four.

Don't make another mistake.

Five.

Let her go.

"I know what you're doing." Ruby crossed her arms, flames blazing in her eyes now. "You're pretending the kiss didn't mean anything."

"We're not going to talk about this now."

"Yes, we are!" Ruby's voice rose above the ticking, above the pounding in Shea's ears, above any last dregs of strength she'd been using to keep herself whole. "Stop pretending like you don't care! Tell me the truth, Shea, *please!*"

"It doesn't matter what I feel." Shea didn't shout back. She was good at not shouting. Good at keeping her voice steely and low when it needed to be, even when she hated herself for it. "You're leaving, and it was just a kiss. There are other things to worry about at the moment."

Ruby huffed in disbelief and shifted on her feet, cheeks drawing in until the hollows were filled with shallows. And then she puffed out another breath, and Shea felt her own spill out of her in unison. She could pretend, but they were still synchronised to the same melody, the same beat.

"Fine. If this is how you want it to be." A step closer and Ruby's breath fanned across Shea's. A rasping, spine-tingling whisper: "But it wasn't just a kiss, Shea. Not for me."

I know. I know what it was. The words clogged in Shea's throat, and she gulped them back down before straightening. "Get dressed. They'll be waiting for you."

She left the bedroom before she did something she'd come to regret. Something like kiss Ruby again. Something like admit that she cared more than she should.

Something like get her heart broken, just as it had been before.

❊ ❊ ❊

Ruby watched Shea shrink in the wing mirror and then disappear, her heart left behind with her. She had tried. She had wanted. She had made it clear to Shea how she felt. It hadn't been enough.

She didn't regret it. She didn't regret kissing Shea. She didn't regret finding something in Shea she hadn't expected to find, beneath all of the taunts and hostility. She just regretted that Shea hadn't given her a chance, and now she had to leave before they'd even had the time to find out what was between them.

"You took the wrong turn there, Claire." Liam's voice sounded muffled to Ruby's ears, just as it had when Ruby had been locked in her grief. She would fight her way out of it alone this time. She knew now that she could.

She glanced out of the tinted windows, uncertain of how much time had passed. Uncertain of where she would go from here. How much longer could she run from whatever sick, twisted thing chased her? How much longer could she be locked away from the world?

"I'll take the next one," Claire replied from the driver's seat, tapping her fingers against the steering wheel.

Liam sighed and turned in his seat, his seatbelt straining against his lean torso. "You all right back there, Rubes?"

Rubes. She hadn't been "Rubes" since Ezra had died, except with Cerys. It felt nice to hear it, and she forced a small smile. "Yeah."

Liam's mirrored smile was sympathetic, as though he knew what was bothering her. Maybe he did. Shea wouldn't have told him, but maybe Claire had after she'd seen them in the kitchen last night. Or maybe it was just written all over Ruby's face. "Where are we going again?"

"Dorset. It's about a six-hour drive. You should try to rest."

The window was cool against Ruby's temple as she leaned against it, though she didn't feel like resting. She didn't feel like doing anything but watch the mottled-grey night bleed into dawn and soak up her last moments with a place that had begun to feel like home.

"Claire." Liam sat forward again, confusion rising in his voice. "Where are you going?"

"Long way 'round," she muttered. "Road-works."

With only his profile visible from the passenger seat, Ruby could only catch a glimpse of his expression — a faint wrinkling of his brow, a vein snaking into his hairline, a quiver in his jaw.

Wordlessly, he pulled his phone from his pocket and typed a message. "Are you sure? I don't think this leads to the motorway."

"I know how to bloody well drive, Liam," Claire huffed. Her voice was so acidic that it burned away any sense of peace Ruby felt a moment before.

Her spine tingling with unease, she craned her neck to peer out of the rear window, frowning when she found that Eric's and Leona's cars were no longer trailing them. Something was wrong, and whatever it was gnawed at her gut. "Where are the others?"

Liam turned too, a storm rolling across his usually calm features. He pressed his phone to his ear, and Ruby could hear the dull dial tone from the backseat.

And then a metallic click.

The nose of a gun was just visible between

the seats. Gripped by Claire. Pointed at Liam. Ruby's heart stuttered to nothing more than a pathetic echo, fear dragging the air from her lungs. Why did Claire have a gun? Why was it pointed at *Liam*?

"They're laying a false trail. They'll catch up. Drop the phone and kick it under your seat."

"Claire—" Liam began to protest.

"*Do it!*"

The shrill demand startled Ruby's pulse back to life. Her fingers clawed at the leather seat padding just for something to grab onto as Liam lifted his free hand with caution and lowered his phone to the floorboard with the other. It slid beneath his seat, into Ruby's view, a moment later.

"What are you doing?" The words had been hiding somewhere in a mess of confusion and fear, but Ruby found them eventually.

"It's nothing personal, Ruby." In the rearview mirror, Claire's eyes remained fixed steadily on the road, the gun remaining tethered to Liam. "Just business."

Liam dared a glance back at her. Ruby searched his eyes for some sort of clue, but they held nothing — a sure sign that something was wrong. Liam's eyes always held *something*: understanding, sympathy, reassurance. All things Ruby needed now more than ever.

"It was you," Liam surmised finally, voice rumbling as loudly as the car motored across the gravelly country lanes. They were going higher, rolling their way through valleys, over lakes, nothing restricting them but low stone walls and the charcoal gun winking at her. Wherever they were going, it wasn't Dorset. "You set this up to get her away from the house."

Claire didn't reply; just took them higher, farther, until the trees were nothing but specks of green and brown and Ruby couldn't imagine ever getting free of the hills and fields and this cursed car.

"Who hired you?"

Hired her? Why would somebody be hired to do this? Why would somebody want Ruby away from the house, away from Shea?

But Claire didn't just want her away from the house or Shea. She had a gun. She was taking them to the middle of nowhere instead of Dorset.

Claire wanted Ruby dead.

The thought didn't summon panic the way Ruby expected it would — only a sinister shiver creeping across her skin, causing her arms to pebble with goosebumps. She was going to die. Somebody wanted her to die. A crazed fan was terrible but not uncommon. All celebrities had their lives threatened. It came with the territory. But somebody wanting her *dead...* somebody setting it all up to do it in the right moment, away from the house, from Shea, planning each step with articulate precision....

Claire had seen Shea and Ruby kissing last night. She knew what was between them, maybe even more than Ruby knew herself. And Ruby had told Shea about Fusion, how they had mistreated the band, driven Ruby to the brink of collapse, how Ezra had wanted to expose them for what they were.

If Claire had been in the house, she would have heard it all. And she didn't work for the Metropolitan Police like Liam. She worked for a private security company hired by Fusion. Somebody had *paid* Claire to get Ruby here. To wipe Ruby from the world along with all of the truth she'd been preparing herself to bring to light. To silence her.

"Fusion," she managed to croak out finally, answering Liam's question though it hadn't been meant for her. "My management. *They* hired you, didn't they?"

"Clever girl," Claire drawled as they slid around a tight corner. The wheels bumped and skidded against loose stone, Ruby's insides rattling with the car.

"Why?" Liam glanced between them wildly, a step behind.

"I admitted to Shea last night that I was thinking about exposing them for mistreatment of their clients. It could have ruined them. It could have ruined me." A thought dawned painfully then, and the colour leached from Ruby's face. "Ezra. Was that… was that planned too?"

"You were both supposed to go down with that bus," Claire said. "I won't make the same mistake twice—"

It happened in a flash of disorienting movement and images: bright grey skies, green hills, all careening past the windows as though they had been dropped from the sky. Ruby was back on the tour bus again, tumbling around the four metal walls and ceiling while she screamed, screamed, screamed. Pain burning holes into her skin and—

Ezra. Where is Ezra?

The seatbelt anchored her this time where he hadn't been able to, but her head skimmed the roof all the same, the wind stolen from her lungs as windows shattered, and it never seemed to stop....

And then it did, all at once. The falling, and the pain, and Ruby. They all stopped, the ground light beneath them and yet somehow heavy enough to drag the car down nose-first. Not soil, not grass.

Water.

The airbags exploded at the front, pinning Liam to his seat. He didn't react, didn't move, blood trickling in a steady stream down the side of his face.

"Liam!" she called desperately. Nothing. Her only real chance of getting out of here, unconscious.

Something cold and wet seeped into her shoes and socks then, drawing a gasp from Ruby's throat. Water pooling into the car. She was running out of time. She tried to open the doors first, but if it was possible, she wasn't strong enough with just one decent arm. She would have to crawl through Claire's shattered window.

Through heaving breaths, Ruby's clumsy fingers fumbled to unbuckle her seatbelt, the water lapping against her ankles. She kicked through it, moving as slowly as she could into the centre seat. Claire was slumped against the cracked window with closed eyes.

The water puddled around Ruby's shins. She was running out of time.

The car rocked with her movements as she rose on unfeeling legs and climbed her way into the front seats. She released Liam from his seatbelt, shaking him but unwilling to call his name again. If Claire woke now, Ruby would be dead before the car sank to the lake's bed.

The gun.

She caught the black barrel between the seats, Claire's fingers still curled around the butt. Ruby's teeth chattered, her body screaming to just get out. But Ruby didn't listen. Steadily, gently, with more calm than Ruby ever knew she could possess, she slid the gun from Claire's grip, remembering how the woman had pointed it at Liam.

For half a moment, Ruby's finger twitched on the trigger.

And then she remembered the iciness seeping through her and found the water at the top of her thighs.

Braver now, she whispered: "Liam. Liam,

wake up." His blood was tacky against her palms as she patted his face desperately. "*Please*, Liam."

But Liam didn't stir, and she didn't have time.

"I'm sorry," she whispered, tears flooding her eyes as she reached over Claire's motionless body to crawl through the shattered window. "I'm so, so sorry."

She slipped awkwardly across Claire, through the gap, with the gun still in her hand.

Her lungs rattled when she sucked in a breath above the surface, the cool air kissing her damp skin and droplets crawling across her face like spiders. She wasn't far from the lake's banks, but any hope that somebody might be waiting, somebody who could help, dissipated as her head darted to gauge her surroundings.

It was more a shallow boggy pond in the middle of fields and hills than a lake. The road Claire had driven off was empty. Ruby had wished to be alone for her entire career, and now she was, head bobbing above murky water and legs kicking against something slimy. It wasn't quite as liberating as she'd hoped.

Behind her, the car groaned and sunk deeper. She could go to the banks now and haul herself out. Run. Maybe find her way back to Shea's farm.

But Liam had been kind to Ruby. He'd been a friend. And he was Shea's friend.

She couldn't just leave him.

Ruby tucked the gun into her waistband, and swam back to the half-submerged car, praying that Claire wouldn't wake up while she wrestled to pull Liam out. She sure as hell wasn't going to let another person go if she could help it. She'd never had the chance to save Ezra, but she had this now, and she wouldn't waste it. She wouldn't have death's arms keep swinging around her neck.

For Liam.
For Shea.
For Ezra.
For herself.

CHAPTER EIGHT

The house felt empty and desaturated without Ruby. Shea couldn't stop thinking about their last conversation, how she had pushed Ruby away. It might have been the last time they'd ever see one another, and Shea had been cold and distant — as distant as she could pretend to be, at least.

Maybe it had been wrong of her, but what else could she have done? One kiss didn't change who they were. A retired officer and a famous musician were hardly a match made in heaven.

She tried not to think about it as she made her way into the security quarters behind the stable. She tried not to think about the feathers sticking to the soles of her boots, either, or the way Flint followed her with his tail limp between his legs as though he knew something was wrong. They had left the office as though they planned on coming back, everything packed up in a rush and paperwork left forgotten. The computer was still locked onto the footage from this morning.

Shea rewound the timer back to three a.m., half an hour before Liam woke her with the news.

There was nothing on the camera outside the stable.

She tried again with the camera tucked above the back door of the main house, the wired edge of the chicken coop just visible at the edge of the frame. Nothing. There was nothing on any of the cameras. Not even the hidden ones, which the intruder couldn't possibly have known existed.

Nothing but — *there*. Shea narrowed her eyes in concentration as she hit pause. The screen stilled on a greyscale image of the backyard, the fence and pigsty silhouetted in the night. And at the corner, a black smudge of movement suspended. A boot.

It should have stepped into frame, but when Shea pressed play, the screen flickered and the boot disappeared. She wondered if she was grasping at straws as she rewound the footage and slowed it down for a second viewing.

She wasn't. There was a boot there one moment, heading in the direction of the camera, and the next it was blipped from existence. Shea knew from her years with the MET that there was only ever one explanation for stilted, nonsensical security footage. Somebody had edited the tape.

She played it back a final time, focusing on the timestamp. It flickered from seventeen minutes past three to half-past. Thirteen minutes unaccounted for. Thirteen minutes that had ended with feathers peppering the grass and the chickens killed and, eventually, Ruby gone.

There were only five people with access to this office. Shea, Liam, Claire, Eric, and Leona.

Claire had been the one working here this morning. Eric had been sleeping in the next room. Liam and Leona had been on watch outside. One of them was lying, or else Claire did not make such a good security guard after all. It took talent to ignore an imposter breaking into the office and deleting footage at her desk, knowing exactly which cameras to avoid and which to wipe.

This wasn't the work of an impulsive, infatuated stalker chasing after Ruby for kicks. This was someone who knew what they were doing. Someone who knew the farm and its security measures. It was one of them. It had to be. But why?

A shrill beep tore Shea from any theories she might have had. Her phone vibrated in the pocket of her jeans, and she pulled it out to check who it was. It was rare that people texted her.

The message was from Liam. Shea unlocked the phone to find not one, but two bubbles on their iMessage thread. The ones before were mostly Liam asking what was for dinner — the man enjoyed her home cooking too much — but this one wasn't about dumplings or pies.

It was three letters: *SOS*. Below, Liam had attached his location, offering Shea an invite to view it. She did, finding a red pin travelling not toward Dorset as it should have been, but further into Cumbria, across fine curling lines that weren't marked with road names or nearby towns. The middle of nowhere.

She remembered saying goodbye to Liam. Watching him get into the passenger side while Claire sat in the driver's seat and Ruby alone in the back. He was with Claire. Heading the wrong way. Asking Shea for help.

"*Shit.*"

The pieces fell together at once, bringing with them a rush of fear that turned Shea cold. And beyond that, adrenaline sparked through her, leaving her joints restless and her teeth gritted. She ceased being *Shea, the retired officer turned farmer*, and went back to that old self, the one who protected and was taught to always be on guard. The one who didn't think, didn't question herself, just acted and helped where it was needed.

And it was needed here, now. For Liam. For Ruby.

Oh, God. Ruby.

Claire had Ruby. Shea had to get to her before anything happened. Everything she cared about was piled into one car with a woman who had lied and snuck around and killed Shea's bloody chickens. She had to get to them.

It took her five minutes to make sure the animals were all secured around the farm. With uncertainty looming over her, she couldn't bear to leave Flint alone, so she locked the house and they ran to Shea's jeep together. Flint climbed into the passenger seat, ears perked up and eyes watching Shea carefully. She petted him — if only to calm her own nerves — drinking in a deep breath before jabbing her keys into the ignition.

"Let's go find them," she whispered. The engine roared to life and dust sprayed beneath the tyres as they launched onto the road.

Shea would do whatever it took to make sure they were safe.

* * *

It turned out that attempting to drag an unconscious man twice Ruby's height out of a pond was no easy feat. Ruby didn't know how long she had been trying, only that the cold had become a part of her now, her muscles cramping in their last feeble attempts to ward it off. Behind them, only the roof of the car was visible, the rest of it underwater and disturbing the muck beneath the surface.

"Come on," she hissed through gritted teeth. Her arms throbbed with the effort of trying to haul Liam up to the banks. *"Please*, Liam." She was so close, so close to getting out, but she couldn't keep going. She couldn't—

A car screeched to a stop on the road above her, the first one she'd seen since the crash. A faded black Jeep. One she knew well. One that left a sob of relief wracking through her tender ribs.

A pale-gold head emerged a moment later.

"Shea," Ruby whispered, her chin dipping beneath the water's surface. And then, louder: "Shea! Down here!"

Shea was already half-running, half-stumbling through the tall blades of grass and flattened wire fences, the worry crumpling her features becoming clear as she grew closer. "Are you okay?"

"I can't—" Ruby slipped beneath the surface again, swallowing a gulp of foul-tasting water and then coughing it back up when she fought her way up. "I can't get him up. I can't—"

"I've got him." Shea crouched at the edge of the water, and Ruby could feel the tears begin to slide down her face again. Tears of relief now, though. Shea was here. Shea had come for her. "Where's Claire?"

Liam's weight lessened against Ruby as Shea curled her hands around his arms.

"The car." Ruby was still gasping for breath, but she slid beneath Liam's arm to help Shea. "It wasn't a stalker, Shea. It was her. She did all of this. She—"

"I know." Shea's voice was strained, and she let out a groan as she tried to pull. But the water made him heavy and he barely rose above the surface. "I need your help to get him up," Shea directed before Ruby could forget where she was, what had happened, what still needed to be done. She braced her legs and wrapped her hands around one upper arm. "Get on his other side."

Ruby waded behind Liam, sucking water from her Cupid's bow, and bent down. He was so heavy now, no longer buoyed by the water. Ruby gripped his shirt, hand stiff with cold. "I don't know if I can."

"You can." Shea's words were firm, the real meaning of them clear as day: not that Ruby could, but that she had to. If she didn't, there was no getting out of this. "On the count of three."

A nod as Ruby adjusted her grip on Liam's shirt. It was slippery with pond muck.

"One," Shea counted. "Two. *Three*."

Water pooled and poured as they both dug into their deepest wells of strength. Everything in Ruby ached as she pulled, hoping to God Shea didn't pull Liam's other arm straight out of his socket. But they made it up onto the banks, Liam falling limp between Shea and Ruby as they collapsed onto the grass for just a moment. The grey clouds rolled and pulsed above Ruby, anchoring her back to earth, back to life. She had been so certain this was the end. She almost died. Almost let Liam die.

"Liam." Shea's voice was full of a panic Ruby hadn't known Shea could possess. It was enough to drive her upright. "Liam, can you hear me?"

Shea clasped her hands together; placed them over Liam's chest.

"Liam." A cry, heartbreaking and raw and piercing.

Ruby held her breath as Shea began compressions, thrusting and begging as her green eyes filled with tears.

Would it always end like this? Somebody dying or dead, somebody lost because of Ruby? Because of who she was and what she wanted? Death and tragedy surrounded her like black smoke, destroying everything she knew, swallowing it, and Ruby couldn't run. She could only watch as Shea tried to pound the life back into her friend.

"Ruby," she huffed, a damp, blonde strand of hair sticking to her face. Dirt and sludge clung to the side of her neck and her arms, her shirt see-through now and clinging to any bit of her it could find. "My phone is in my car. I need you to call an ambulance."

Dazed and hopeless and angry, Ruby could only nod and pull herself up to feet that no longer wanted to work. She stumbled, following the tyre-trampled tracks back up the hill—

And halting. Another car had finally appeared on the long-empty road, about two miles behind them and moving faster than it should, considering the terrain. No, not a car; an SUV with the same headlamp configuration as the one she'd too recently escaped. It would be on them in a minute, maybe less.

Her heart pounded, through her ears and her chest and her toes. "They've found us." She turned around, and Shea stopped compressions to glance up at Ruby. "They've found me, Shea. They're going to kill me."

Shea's lips parted, her eyes arcing past Ruby to the new threat.

"They're going to kill me," Ruby whispered again, this time to herself. It was never-ending.

They would never stop. She would never be safe.

"No." Shea stiffened defiantly, her pale lashes fanning high, flushed cheekbones as she glanced down to sweep her hand across Liam's bloodied head. It was the only moment she allowed herself before she was on her feet and grabbing Ruby's hand. "No, they're not."

"Shea—" Ruby didn't know how the sentence was supposed to end. She didn't know anything. Liam was still on the ground and the car was coming and Claire was sinking somewhere in that pond, lungs probably already saturated with water, and Shea's fingers were threaded through her own and pulling her up like a rope tossed from a ship to a passenger who had fallen overboard.

Ruby clung to that rope with every bit of strength she had left. She let Shea pull her away from the wreckage she had caused, forced her eyes on the Jeep rather than the SUV that would be close enough to spot them in just a few seconds, and let Shea cram her into the passenger seat with Flint waiting for them as she rounded to the driver's side and searched for her phone.

She barely heard the conversation Shea had over the phone, too wary of the storm closing in on them. It barely lasted a minute, but it felt like hours.

Shea locked the doors and thrust on her seatbelt before starting the car. "Put your seatbelt on."

Ruby barely heard her. She wasn't here. She

was somewhere else, still underwater maybe, with no way out. But then there was her name, passing from lips she had kissed last night. There was that hoarse, Irish voice. There was Shea's palm, rough and icy against Ruby's cheek, brushing away the hairs and the dirt and the fear.

"We don't have time, Ruby. Are you hurt?"

There was Flint's tongue swiping at the grass and moss sticking to her clothes, and there was Shea closer, closer, keeping her safe when she should have been with her friend, with Liam. "No. No, I don't think so."

It was the truth. Her neck ached and her temple was tender, but that was all she felt.

Shea inspected her only a nanosecond longer, and Ruby locked herself on those concerned green eyes. And then Shea reached over to strap her in. Ruby finished the job, clicking the buckle into place, their trembling fingers brushing for half a second.

It was all Ruby needed.

"They're going to follow us," Shea said steadily, glancing in the rearview mirror as the car rumbled back onto the path. She accelerated, too fast for a country road and a beaten-down truck. "But once we get back onto the road, it's going to be fine. They won't risk being seen by anyone else. I want you to tell me everything you know. Don't focus on them."

Ruby watched the black SUV follow them in the rearview mirror, and she told Shea the truth, even if she didn't quite know what it was.

And for the first time, she was glad Ezra wasn't alive to see what her life had turned into.

CHAPTER NINE

They lost the SUV somewhere in Carlisle. After Ruby told Shea about Claire, Shea drove in silence for a long time. She didn't know where she was taking them. They couldn't go home. They couldn't stop moving at all, not for long. And Shea couldn't let herself think about Liam lying on the marshy banks, his chest too still and his eyes fused shut. So she stared at the road ahead and she pretended she knew what she was doing for Ruby's sake.

Even after all these years, her first instinct was to call her ex-partner Kate. They needed somebody they could trust. Somebody who couldn't be touched by Fusion's money and corruption. Kate was the only person Shea could think of, but as far as she knew, she was in London now. Shea was just trying to get out of Cumbria in one piece.

She'd dumped her phone with Liam anyway, that way the ambulance would find him. The only other problem was the Jeep. Shea didn't doubt that they would find them again as long as she stayed in a recognisable car. After three hours of travelling at the speed limit down the M6, she gave in and pulled into a service station.

"Ten minutes," Shea said, eyeing the gash on Ruby's temple warily. She was lucky that was all the crash left behind. Still, her skin was a ghastly grey and her eyes were wide, panicked. Her hair had dried in untamed curls. Flint was comfortably sprawled across the backseat, oblivious to their troubles. "It's all we can afford. They'll have people trying to track us down everywhere. They've made an attempt on your life. They won't risk letting you escape now."

Ruby licked her chapped bottom lip, brows knitting together. "Shouldn't we call the police?"

"We're going to." Shea drummed her fingertips against the steering wheel nervously. She hadn't spoken to Kate since she'd woken in the hospital, unable to move, unable to feel her feet. But Shea would never forget the way Kate had looked at her. The disappointment and the shame and the anger.

"And then what?"

Shea shook her head and mumbled, "I don't know."

She hated to admit it. It felt as though the world was built from barbs and closing in on them. But she wasn't worried for herself. She was worried for Ruby, for what they would do to her. They'd tried to kill her twice. Shea couldn't let them try for a third.

Ruby sighed and put her head in her hands. "They killed Ezra, Shea."

"I know." Shea reached her hand out, tracing

delicate circles across Ruby's taut shoulder blades. Her jumper was still coarse with damp, and Shea could smell the rancid pond water on them both, clinging to their hair, their skin. Shea had a feeling they wouldn't get rid of it any time soon.

"They'll kill me."

"*No*." Her voice stabbed through the eerie quiet, defiant and blazing. "I won't let that happen."

Ruby lifted her gaze, brown eyes swirling with tears — whiskey diluted with water. "You left Liam."

"I know." It was killing Shea. She didn't know what would happen to him. If he was alive. He wasn't breathing when they left him.

The guilt made Shea ache. She wrapped her arms across her torso and pressed her head back into the seat. "Fuck."

"Fuck," Ruby agreed. And then, after moments of nothing but the light spit of rain pattering against the windowpane: "How did you find me?"

"Liam. He sent me your location."

"And you came." Her voice was light with disbelief, and when Shea looked at her, she found her features heavy with it.

"Of course I came," Shea said it quietly, not something she wanted to admit. She couldn't afford to care now. But she couldn't help it either.

Ruby's hand drifted past the gearstick between them and found Shea's, their pinky fingers brushing. Shea almost leaned in, almost told her how world-endingly worried she had been when she found out that Ruby was in danger, almost kissed her to prove it.

But now wasn't the time.

"Just out of curiosity, what's your stance on car theft?" She diverted her attention back to the service station, the car park. It was half-full: plenty of choices.

Wariness twisted across Ruby's features. "Why?"

Shea shrugged casually, her focus following a suited middle-aged man who was getting out of a gunmetal-grey Mazda. He slid his keys into the pocket of his long, expensive-looking coat and disappeared into the service station.

Target acquired.

"We need to switch cars so that there's less chance of us being found."

"So we're going to *steal* one?"

"Do you have any better ideas?"

Ruby's bottom lip jutted into a pout. "No, I suppose not."

"Good. Off we go then." Shea flashed her a smile with more confidence than she felt, opening the glove compartment to find the baseball cap she usually wore to shield her face from the summer heat and handing it to Ruby. "Just don't let anyone recognise you, please."

"That's it?" Ruby glowered at the pale-blue cap as though it might contain lice. "No plan?"

"We don't have time. Here." Shea's purse came next; she emptied the loose coins into her hand before handing it over. "You get us a few supplies in the shop — cash *only* — and then come back out to get Flint. I'll do the hard stuff. I need to make a call first though."

"You're serious, aren't you?"

"Deadly."

Incredulous, Ruby huffed — and then hesitated. "Then I have something for you too." She shifted to pull something out of the waistband of her jeans, hidden beneath her jumper. A gun. Shea's heart almost broke out of her ribs. "I took it from Claire. It got wet, so...."

When her finger hovered too close to the trigger, Shea tugged it away, put the safety on, and concealed it in her own waistband. Before she could fall prisoner to the phantom shots firing in her ears, echoes of the sounds she'd heard that night, she opened the car door and jumped down. "Let's not play with guns. Come on."

The flat concrete was at least better than the uneven farmland and hills and pond banks from earlier. Summoning false confidence, Shea threw the keys of the Jeep over the bumper to Ruby and sauntered into the station without a second glance back. Out of all the things Ruby had been through today, this would surely be the easiest to handle. Her only job was to buy supplies and collect Flint. Meanwhile, Shea needed to find the fancy Mazda Man, who, by the looks of the tailored coat and trousers he'd worn, could certainly manage without a twenty-grand car.

The place was more a food court than anything else. Ruby passed by Shea to head into WH Smith, and Shea wandered slowly over to the telephone by KFC. Her fingers flexed over the numbers after slotting in the right change. Did she even *know* Kate's number?

She shouldn't have remembered — and yet, after dropping in the coins, it came to her one digit at a time, memorised from three years of looking her up online and wishing she had a right to call. The keys were cold against her fingertips, and she had to be careful not to touch a questionable yellow stain that Shea hoped was mustard on the phone itself as she picked it up.

While the phone dialled, Shea searched for Mazda Man, fighting the jitters snaking through her stomach with a few deep breaths. God, how had she gotten here? Twelve hours ago, the only thing she had to worry about was kissing the celebrity living in her safe house. Now she was on the bloody run with her.

There was no sign of him yet, and the phone rang for so long that any hope of getting Kate's help dwindled. She would have to do this on her own, keep Ruby safe alone—

"Hello?"

"Oh, *shit*," Shea cursed without thought and then covered her mouth. She really hadn't been prepared for an answer. "Shit, sorry. Is this Kate

Wilde?"

"Shea O'Connor?" The voice was as familiar to Shea as the pattern on her mother's painted china set in the farmhouse kitchen, clipped and clear and married to memories of a stiff blue collar biting into Shea's neck, and a hail of gunfire that ended with fiery, agonising pain shooting through her back. Kate. Shea had thrown herself in front of bullets for Kate, and now she couldn't even bloody well say "hello" like a half-normal person.

"Am I that recognisable?" she managed to stutter out.

"Not many people answer the phone by cursing."

Shea sucked in a breath, imagining Kate with her phone pressed between her ear and shoulder, a black coffee on her desk. "Right. Sorry."

"It's…." Kate cleared her throat; paused. "It's been a while."

"It has, and I wouldn't call if I had any other option." Shea's knuckles turned white around the black phone, the plastic receiver digging into her palms. "But I need your help."

Pathetic. Shea sounded pathetic. Grovelling to a woman who didn't want anything to do with her. A woman who Shea had almost died for. A woman who had turned her away, rejected her.

But it was for Ruby. She had to do it for Ruby.

Kate must have heard the desperation in Shea's tone, because she asked, "What is it?"

"It's… look, it's a long story. A woman who's

been staying at the farm with me is in some really big trouble. The people supposed to be protecting her were actually hired to kill her, and now we're on the run."

"Jesus," Kate breathed. "It's never a dull moment with you, is it?"

"Can you help us?"

"I… I'm a detective now, but yes. Yes, I think I can help you. Tell me more."

A detective. It was what Kate had always wanted to do. Maybe Shea should have felt pride, or maybe she should have been impressed, but she didn't feel much of anything and—

There. Mazda Man queuing at Starbucks across the court, checking his wristwatch as though waiting for the luxury of a five-pound coffee was an inconvenience. Shea kept her gaze fixed on him as she spoke.

"Her name is Ruby Bright. The people trying to kill her are her management team, Fusion. She was going to expose them for their mistreatment of clients, so they're trying to silence her before it gets out and they lose everything. They're a multi-million company, so I have no idea how widespread this is, how many people are after us. I just…." Her eyes fluttered shut for a second as she thought about Ruby. Ruby arriving at the farmhouse with bruised ribs and a broken arm that was still covered in a cast. Ruby telling Shea the truth about being a musician, giving so much of herself that there was nothing left. Ruby having to live with the knowledge that they had killed her best friend. Ruby thrashing with Liam in her arms in that pond while the car supposed to keep her safe sank behind her. "I need her safe, Kate. I don't know how to keep her safe."

A sigh quivered across the line. "You always know how to keep people safe, Shea. You always have."

Shea wished that were true, but they both knew it wasn't. It was unusual for Kate to lie through her teeth.

"Is it just the two of you?"

"Yeah."

"Where are you now?"

She glanced for a clue, the name of the service station, a map; found it printed across the back wall beside Burger King. "Stoke-on-Trent."

"All right. I can pull some strings, but you know as well as I do that we can't rely on the MET for stuff like this. If Fusion holds as much power as you think, nobody can be trusted. Can you get her to London? To me?"

"Yeah, I can get us there." Weariness weighed down on Shea as she directed her gaze back to Mazda Man. He sipped his coffee; content and apparently not in a rush after all, since he also had a sandwich and cake laid out on a table and had pulled out his laptop. "It's going to involve some grand theft auto."

"I'd expect nothing less; but for the sake of my career, I'm going to pretend I didn't hear that."

Kate almost sounded proud, though that was ridiculous. "I'm about to head out of the office, and I won't be back until tonight. The best thing you can do today is lie low. Drive a few more hours and then dump the car, find a bus or a train to a small town nobody would think to look in, get some rest in a B&B that takes cash. No using phones or credit cards that can be traced back to either of you. Find me tomorrow; my office is in the New Scotland Yard building."

"All right. Okay." Shea blew out a relieved breath. The plan had been building itself on the edge of her mind, anyway, but it was reassuring to know she had at least one person on their side. One person who wasn't trying to kill them. "Thanks, Kate."

"Stay safe, Shea."

Shea couldn't make that promise. She slammed the phone back into the receiver and swallowed down her fear. There wasn't enough time to let it escape. She had a job to do and a car to steal.

A moment later, Ruby emerged from the shop with her head bowed and a plastic bag in her hand. She sent Shea a nod as she passed and then left through the revolving doors. Shea watched her retreat across the grey car park and then free Flint from the Jeep.

It was Shea's turn now. She idled over to Starbucks with her hands in her pockets, making sure Mazda Man's back remained to her so that he wouldn't catch sight of her yet. The less of Shea he saw, the better. His coat had been draped over the chair, his chiselled reflection just visible on the screen of his laptop. Shea scoured the right-hand pocket and prayed to God the keys were still in there.

And then she knelt with one remaining one-pound coin in one hand, the other snaking into the man's coat pocket to gather the keys. Jagged metal teeth bit into her palm, her hands curling around the pebble shape of the push-button. *Thank the heavens.*

"Excuse me, sir?" Shea snatched the keys and placed them in the pocket of her jacket just before Mazda Man turned around. A dried blueberry lingered like a mole at the corner of his mouth. "I think you dropped some change."

The man eyed the coin as though it had been pulled out of a steaming pile of animal faeces instead of just a mildly dirty floor, his hazel-eyed gaze studying Shea from head to toe once over. Shea thought for a moment that he knew, but then he sniffed and said, "Keep it."

With a smug smile, he went back to typing on his laptop, biting the corner of his sandwich as he did. Clearly, he thought he'd done his good deed for the day. *Snob.*

The keys burned a hole into Shea's pocket as she grinned back politely and rose to her haunches before wandering away.

At least *something* had gone to plan today.

CHAPTER TEN

They dumped the stolen Mazda on the side of a random road in Wolverhampton and then caught three trains in twice as many hours. Ruby didn't have time to be afraid or anxious. She didn't have time for anything but the running and the shifting from station to station, platform to platform, train to train. Shea kept her hand in Ruby's, kept her steady and here, clasp only ever getting stronger when Ruby's own weakened.

Flint at least seemed to be enjoying the journey, especially when they arrived in a small village called Alvechurch under darkening, cloud-freckled, three o'clock skies and set off on foot. Good. Nausea was beginning to twist through Ruby's gut again. She couldn't handle any more travelling today.

Shea slowed as they ambled down country roads, past grassy fields, Flint stopping occasionally to study the grazing cows. His tail wagged as though he thought they might be his friends from the farm in Cumbria.

"What now?" Ruby's voice was hoarse. They'd barely spoken since abandoning the car. She hadn't even asked who Shea had called in the service station, and Shea hadn't offered up the information. Not that she was usually one for transparency anyway. Still, it was getting cold, and Ruby's mouth felt as though thick sand had been shovelled into it, and she wasn't sure how much longer she could keep moving without taking a few breaths first. She could still taste pond water in her mouth. Needed to wash it out so that she wouldn't have to keep thinking of Liam and Claire and the gun and the almost drowning.

Shea nodded straight ahead, eyes narrowed and mouth a thin line. "I saw a sign for a bed and breakfast up this way. We'll stay here for the night and head to London in the morning."

"And then?"

"And then we get help."

Ruby wondered how Shea did it: remained so detached, so emotionless, so unbothered by it all. She was glad for it, glad for that steadfast, unrelenting presence beside her that kept them both standing and moving and safe, but Ruby wished she didn't feel like the only one afraid. She wished Shea would *look* at her, give her some inkling of how bad this was. Ruby didn't need a stiff-spined officer now. She needed Shea. She needed the glimpses of hidden softness or the blazing concern Ruby had seen after the crash. She needed to know she cared enough not to give up on her as everybody else had.

She just *needed*.

In the end, they did find a B&B at the end

of the lane, but not before the heavens opened and drenched them from head to toe. They ran across gravel and over puddles, Ruby just barely having the time to glimpse the name of the place they would stay tonight: The Elm Tree Inn. The building was a patchwork of uneven cobblestones bleeding with wilting wildflowers and ivy. Only two cars were parked outside, and Ruby hoped that meant less chance of being recognised. She had been lucky so far only because nobody expected to see a well-known singer supposed to be recovering from a tour bus accident in random cities on random trains. Shea's tatty cap helped, too.

When they reached the door, they stepped into warm, cinnamon-kissed air and golden light. Ruby wiped her sodden boots on the trodden-down welcome mat at her feet, flinching when Flint violently shook the rain from his fur coat and gave the rest of them a final shower in the process. A sharp gasp cut through the muted pattering of rain, and Ruby winced, heart stuttering, as she waited for the inevitable.

But she lifted her head to find only a middle-aged woman rounding a small desk, her slightly wrinkled hands pressed to her mouth. "Oh, you poor things, getting caught in such an awful downpour! Come in, come in."

"Are dogs all right in here?" Shea asked as the woman ushered them into the foyer. A fire roared in the next room, a staircase spiralling beyond it, but there wasn't another soul in sight.

For the first time in well over twelve hours, Ruby felt safe.

"Of course! What a lovely, fluffy thing he is." The inn owner bent down to fuss over Flint, scratching between his ears as he panted lovingly. She didn't seem to mind the smell of wet dog filling her B&B. "I'll get the two of you some towels, shall I?"

"That would be great, thank you." Shea swept a clump of damp blonde hair from her face, droplets of rain zigzagging down her coat sleeves. "Do you have any vacancies?"

"Oh, yes, we always have room in this inn." The owner grinned and disappeared into a corridor behind the desk. She emerged a moment later with a tower of velvety, duck-egg-blue towels. "Just the one night?"

"Yes, please."

"And are we sharing a room and bed?" A smirk played on the woman's thin lips as she glanced between them suggestively. If Ruby hadn't been preoccupied with a threat to her life, she might have blushed. As it was, she sidled closer to Shea, knowing that as long as they acted naturally, the woman would have no need to question them.

"Anything you have is grand," Shea replied nonchalantly.

"I'll tell you what." The woman rattled something in a hidden desk and then lifted her hand to reveal a key pinched between her fingers. "I'll take the details down once you're all dried off. Give me your coats and bring down your wet clothes when you're done, and I'll pop them in the dryer for you."

"Oh… we don't… well, it was a bit of a spontaneous trip." Shea offered a wry smile, and despite having already watched her steal a car in broad daylight, Ruby was impressed by the subtle act. "We don't really have any spare clothes."

"Not to worry; I'm sure I can find something for you both," the woman dismissed with a bat of her hand. "I'll fetch something up once you're all settled. There's a kettle in the room and dinner is in three hours if you fancy it. My name's Bridget, by the way. Bridge is fine, too, and my friends sometimes just call me B."

Bridget was a woman of many words, Ruby found out as she led them up the stairs to their room. In fact, by the time they stepped into their shelter for the night, Ruby had found out that Bridget was a mother of four sons, a former flight attendant, and somehow had a licence to fly helicopters.

"Well, thank you ever so much, Bridget." Shea pasted a false smile on her face, her hand hovering over the bronze doorknob to prevent Bridget from coming in with them. "We'll be down soon."

Bridget clicked her fingers. "And I'll leave some clothes outside your room for you. *Do* make sure to dry off. We don't want you getting the sniffles."

"We will."

"And let me know if I can get anything for your lovely fur baby here—"

"Yes, bye, Bridget." Shea swung the door shut with a final huff and then pressed her forehead into the wood. "Give me strength," Ruby thought she heard Shea whisper under her breath.

Ruby would need more than strength to get through the rest of the evening. Still, she was grateful for the peace as she shucked off her soggy coat and boots to collapse onto the bed. Her head spun, the geometric pattern printed on the ceiling distorting itself until she had to close her eyes against it. The bendy lines were still visible beneath her lids.

"All right, Flint," Shea sighed. "Let's get you dry."

For the next five minutes, Ruby watched through barely open eyes, too exhausted to even try to help, as Shea wrestled with Flint, attempting to bundle the black Labrador in towels. It kept her distracted enough from the shadows lurking in her mind, especially when Flint's tongue painted a line down the centre of Shea's face and the corner of Shea's mouth dimpled with a secret smile. It was strange seeing her somewhere other than the farm. She was still Shea here: still quiet and closed off with something exhilarating and fierce and otherworldly simmering just beneath the surface; still the only thing anchoring Ruby to the world, keeping her from getting lost in all of the things that could hurt her, kill her; still keeping her safe.

A knock at the door set Flint off barking. Shea rose from her kneeling position and opened it, murmuring, "thank you," before returning with a pile of dry clothes — all of which looked dangerously floral.

Shea pulled the gun from her waistband first and stowed it away in the drawer. Ruby pretended the sight didn't leave her uneasy, instead picking her way through daisy-patterned pinafores and perfume-drowned blouses until she found a pair of dungarees and a colourful cardigan.

Though not very subtle for a woman on the run, it would have to do.

She didn't bother going into the bathroom to change. There was nothing that Shea had already seen of Ruby that was worse than her bare, bruised body — and a part of her *wanted* to show it. To show she didn't care, to see what Shea's reaction would be. To remind Shea that before all of this insanity, an offer had been put on the table. So, Ruby stood, pulled off her jeans, pried her jumper from her skin, and waited for Shea to turn around and look at her. The vanity mirror displayed both of their frames as Shea tied up her hair... and stilled.

Their eyes snagged on one another's, a tangle of reflections until Ruby didn't know which version of Shea was real, or which version of herself was. She only knew that those piercing green eyes found hers and something flickered in them. Something Ruby wanted to see again. Something hot and hungry.

And then it was gone. Shea cleared her throat and threw Ruby a towel before searching the pile of clothes for something to wear herself. Each option caused a grimace, Ruby noticed as she dried herself off and then stepped into the dungarees.

Finally, Shea came to a cream-coloured turtleneck. Despite it being twice the size of her, she peeled off her wet clothes anyway, flashing glimpses of pale skin and narrow hips, toned stomach and a landscape of mountains tattooed on her ribs, taking just long enough that Ruby knew Shea didn't mind her seeing, either. It was a good job; Ruby couldn't take her eyes off her, couldn't stop imagining what it would feel like to trace the endless shapes of a body that had endured more than Ruby could imagine. Her lips tingled with want, and that want slithered down through her chest to the pit of her stomach. Scars and bruises, ink and beauty spots — Ruby wanted to paint them all with kisses and touches.

A blush blossomed across Ruby's face when Shea's eyes met hers, the confidence tugged from her in an instant until she had to avert her gaze. When Shea plunged into the oversized jumper, the sleeves drowned her hands and the high neckline sagged around the lack of anything to hug.

Ruby had never seen Shea look small before, but she did now as she rolled up the sleeves, fibres of wool sticking to her damp skin. She was lean and not as tall as Ruby, but she marched around the farm with so much confidence and power that it was easy to forget that, really, Shea was just an average-framed person rather than an all-powerful, flannel-wearing giant or a human shield.

That wasn't to say Ruby doubted Shea. She had a heart made for fighting, and an oversized jumper didn't change that.

"Who did you call at the service station earlier?" Ruby dared ask finally, buttoning the straps of her dungarees over a plain white shirt before sinking into the cardigan. The smell of lavender clung to it and, for just a moment, Ruby allowed the comfort to take over. It reminded her of summer evenings spent in her aunt's garden with the kids, long bubble baths when she had the time to come home and take them. Home. She missed home. She wondered if word had gotten back to her aunt yet and could only hope that Fusion would leave her family out of their plots to wipe Ruby from existence. It made her ache to think of it any other way.

"An old friend," Shea muttered quietly, shimmying out of her jeans and swapping the thin black denim for pleated trousers that required the aid of her leather belt. "She's a detective. She can help us. We'll go to her first thing tomorrow."

Ruby nodded, focus drawn to the pastel-blue telephone on the nightstand. She could call her aunt. Knew her number by heart. And Cerys; she needed to call Cerys to figure out if her manager was in on Fusion's plan or if it went well beyond her. She might have been a pain in the arse to work with, but Ruby had seen her as a friend all the same and couldn't imagine the bubbly woman being part of such an awful scheme.

She couldn't help but inch toward the phone, her fingers coiling in the wire.

"You can't call anyone, Ruby," Shea spoke softly enough that Ruby couldn't help but turn around. She found sympathy in Shea's expression, her green eyes gleaming in the dull evening light. "It isn't safe."

"They wouldn't find us *here*, surely?"

Shea shrugged. "I don't know. They're looking for us. We don't know who or how many. We only know they want you gone, and they won't stop now. It's not a chance we can take. Besides, you'd be putting whoever you plan on calling in danger too."

Ruby's bones turned to lead all at once. She slumped back onto the bed, scraping her shaking hands through her dripping mop of dark hair and gazing absently at the black clouds lapping across the pink sky outside.

"It'll be over tomorrow." Shea's voice echoed from the bathroom over running water. "We just have to get you to London, and then it's over."

Would it be? Ruby couldn't imagine it ever being over, not after three years of tour buses and screaming and not being able to walk down Oxford Street without someone calling her name or taking a video of her without her knowing. It had been long and difficult and exhausting, and Ruby had been trapped for so long that she wouldn't recognise freedom even if it found her.

The mattress sank beside Ruby. Shea, sitting down, a damp face cloth in her hand. "Can I take a look at that gash?"

Ruby's fingers lifted midway to her face. She had forgotten about the wound at her temple, had forgotten that the crash was just this morning. A throb came with the remembering and she nodded.

Shea didn't stay on the bed. She crouched between Ruby's knees, crooked teeth tucked behind her bottom lip as she brushed Ruby's hair from her face. Even now, Ruby couldn't stop looking at her, couldn't stop feeling that kiss they'd shared last night. Shea rose higher on her knees until her sharp elbows brushed the inside of Ruby's thighs, making her burn in places she hadn't for a while. So close. So close that they were melding into each other, slotting together, and Ruby could feel every edge and corner where their bodies met.

As Shea pressed the damp cloth to Ruby's temple and dabbed carefully, Ruby's eyes fluttered shut. It was tender, but nothing compared to what she had endured after the tour bus crash — physically *and* emotionally. It was the cold that bothered her more, still locked away in her bones. It felt permanent.

"Looks okay. More bruised than anything," Shea commented, drawing the cloth away. Ruby opened her eyes and saw only a few specks of blood on the fibres. "How's it feel?"

"Fine." Ruby's throat felt full of something she couldn't name, and the words had to slip through serrated spaces to be heard.

"Yeah? What about the rest of you?"

"I'm okay. Not supposed to get my cast wet, though." She gestured wryly with her sodden, plastered arm, which had been chafing and tingling with all the damp it had absorbed today. Though irritating, it was low on Ruby's list of priorities.

"Bet half a lake'll pour out of that thing when it comes off."

A chuckle, shared until Ruby didn't know where hers ended and Shea's began. All she knew was that they were still close, their noses inches away from brushing, and Shea hadn't pulled away yet.

When it comes off, Shea had said. Not *if.* As though she had no doubt they would get through this, to a place where Ruby could walk around without the deadweight on her arm. It made Ruby hope too.

"Shea," she whispered and wasn't quite sure why. Sometimes it felt comforting just to say her name — just to remind herself that she was here, looking after her, keeping her safe.

Shea's hands crawled to the nape of Ruby's neck, urging her face closer still. A wicked, teasing game, because all Ruby wanted to do was close the distance between them, to seek Shea's comfort in the most basic and intimate of ways.

"We're going to be okay." As though Shea knew what Ruby was thinking. As though she could see it written all over Ruby's face. "I Promise."

Show me, Ruby wanted to beg. *Show me we're going to be okay. Promise me with kisses. Let me in again. Let me stay this time.*

There was something familiar and yet new in Shea's words, in the way she looked at Ruby with her chin set and her eyes unblinking. So bold. So certain. Ezra's voice echoed in Ruby's head: *you and me against the world.*

That's what it felt like. Like it was them now against everyone. And Ruby didn't doubt Shea would fight for her. She had already proven it. She had found her when Ruby hadn't asked. She had brought her here as though it was second nature to keep Ruby safe.

Shea dipped her head making to leave, but Ruby couldn't let her. Not now. Not when they were so close. Ruby's selfish fingers clawed through the chunky-knit of Shea's borrowed jumper, keeping her for herself. "Kiss me again, Shea."

Ruby heard Shea's breath snag in her throat. She saw the way her lips parted in surprise. She begged inwardly for Shea to just do it, just let her in, let her stay.

"I can't." Shea's face shuttered, but she didn't

move. Ruby loosened her hands just slightly to test her, to see if she would take the freedom and leave, yet still, Shea stayed locked between her legs. "Not like this."

"Not like what?"

A swallow bobbed in Shea's throat. "You're grieving. You're going through hell."

Ruby's brows drew together. "So?"

"So I'm not a distraction, Ruby, and I won't kiss you every time you need one."

"Is that what you think?" The force of Ruby's words, the sudden anger saturating them, almost choked her.

"Is it not the truth?"

"No!" No hesitation. No pause to wonder. Ruby wasn't broken. Her desire wasn't based on her pain. They were two separate entities, a paradox co-existing inside her. "God, Shea, I can grieve and be afraid and still *want* you — really, truly want you, and not just because I'm hurting. In fact, you're the only person who made me feel like I was still a person. You didn't treat me like a fucking shattered glass bowl wrapped in newspaper. Don't start now. Please don't start—"

Shea silenced Ruby's pleas with her lips, and Ruby gasped, electricity sparking through her. It shouldn't have been possible to feel like this after such an awful day. Ruby had spent her life feeling as though death followed her everywhere, more now than ever — and yet, Shea was the most alive person she'd ever met, and she was kissing her, giving Ruby that life too, and it didn't make sense but Ruby couldn't *stop* feeling Shea in her veins, in her blood, in her bones. She wanted to feel her everywhere else too, and she pulled Shea by the comically oversized turtleneck at her throat so that they could shuffle down the bed; so that Shea could hover on top of her and kiss her deeper, harder, her thighs between Ruby's and her teeth grazing, lips roving all over her, but not enough, not yet.

"That didn't take a lot of convincing," Ruby found it in her to murmur breathlessly, peppering kisses behind Shea's ear, across her sharp jaw, in the small cleft of her chin.

Shea's hands roamed lower, across Ruby's ribs, her soft stomach, her wide hips. "I stole a car today, love. I think at some point we have to say 'fuck it.'"

Love. Ruby loved it when Shea called her that, even when she meant it as a sarcastic quip or a cutting insult. And she loved how Shea had emerged from that service station, keys to a stolen car dangling from her fingers as though they were just something that had fallen into her hands by sheer luck. She loved finding out more about Shea through all of this chaos and madness, loved knowing that Shea could take care of them with skills and talents Ruby didn't know anyone could possess.

"The grand theft auto thing was hot," Ruby admitted, lips sinking into the hollow of Shea's collarbone.

Another rap at the door cleaved them apart. Flint howled, and above the earsplitting noise, Bridget's voice drifted into the room. "Everything all right in there, lovelies?"

Shea groaned out her frustration, head bowing to rest against Ruby's shoulder. Ruby couldn't help but let out a disconcerting laugh.

"Everything's fine, Bridget!" Shea called.

"Oh, fabulous. You'll bring your clothes down and join us for dinner then? My wife made toad-in-the-hole!"

"Yes, Bridget, sounds lovely!"

Ruby wrinkled her nose — it did not sound lovely — and savoured a final, lingering kiss with Shea before she pulled away to thrust her feet back into fresh socks and her old boots. When Ruby followed, examining her wound in the mirror on her way, she found her lips swollen and her chest heaving breathlessly.

If Shea O'Connor kept kissing her, she might just keel over in pieces before Fusion had a chance to find her.

* * *

"Are you awake?"

Shea groaned out a no in response to Ruby's whispered words. She had been dozing, wrapped in the warm, fuzzy promise of much-needed sleep. They hadn't needed to talk much at dinner — Bridget did enough for all of them, and she'd doted on Flint until he rolled over onto his back beneath the dinner table, belly full of sausages and gravy. He lay at their feet now, dead to the world after a long day of travelling.

They hadn't kissed again. Shea still didn't know if she'd done the right thing in letting it happen. She was learning that there was no *right thing* with Ruby. They just *were*, and Shea wasn't strong enough to resist that pull to her any longer. Her head was a mess and she was exhausted from trying to maintain her façade of fearlessness for Ruby's sake. She would figure out the rest when this was over but, tonight, she wouldn't keep pretending that she didn't feel something; that Ruby didn't make her heart flap about in her chest like one of the pigeons always getting caught in the farmhouse chimney. She might have been strong enough to drag Ruby to safety, navigating a minefield of corruption in the process, but Shea wasn't strong enough to stop wanting her.

"Liar." Beside Shea, Ruby shifted onto her side to face her, hand tucked under her head and eyes burning a hole into the side of Shea's cheek.

Shea pretended not to notice, staring up at the shadows curling across the ceiling, her arms planted firmly by her sides. "Go to sleep, Ruby. You need it. We both do."

A sigh whispered from Ruby's lips, and then they fell back into silence, back into the strange comfort of just existing in the same space, the same bed, under the same heavy blanket that reeked of potpourri.

And then a tingle lanced from the crown of her head to her chin. Ruby was the cause, her finger delicately tracing the outline of Shea's face. Shea couldn't remember the last time anybody had touched her that way: like she was fragile and dainty and needed to be handled with the utmost care. She liked being strong, but she needed this reminder tonight. She needed it from Ruby. She could be soft too. She could be treated with tenderness too.

"I don't think I can sleep," Ruby admitted, her breath fanning across Shea's face. Shea opened her eyes to find Ruby propped up on her pillow, watching her. "Not until this is over."

"Tomorrow." Shea flipped over to lie on her stomach, brushing her knuckles across the subtle swell of Ruby's cheek. She just couldn't bloody well stop herself. "It'll be over tomorrow."

Even in the darkness, Ruby was beautiful: all round lines and glistening eyes, a slither of moonlight slicing across her bare shoulder like a knighting sword. A birthmark darkened the hollow beneath her collarbone, a tempting golden patch of skin left bare from the loose shirt slipping down. Shea imagined kissing it. Imagined kissing all of her. She licked her lips and glanced away before she gave in.

But Ruby sidled closer still, her fingers waltzing down the stairwell of Shea's spine, down, down, down, until they reached that sensitive patch of scar tissue just above her dimples of Venus. It was second nature for Shea to tense, especially since it had only ever been doctors examining her injuries there before now.

Ruby's fingers stilled, her brows sinking together. "Can I?"

Hesitantly, Shea nodded. Ruby crept beneath the hem of Shea's jumper and ran over the uneven skin; all that was left of the three bullets that had buried themselves in Shea. The stamped memory of the worst time in Shea's life.

"If I ask you what happened, would you tell me?" Ruby questioned.

No. It was Shea's first response, a mechanism well and truly engrained to keep everybody at arm's length. Some of her old friends wore scars like Olympic medals — with pride, with confidence — but Shea wasn't proud of the person she'd become after the incident. She wasn't proud of who the bullets had made her or, rather, what they had unleashed in her. Bitterness. Fear. Disgust.

But then she thought of Ruby sitting at her kitchen table with a glass of wine in her hand, telling Shea all about Fusion and the way they had treated her. Of how she had worked herself to the bone to distract from the grief, how she had always been open, honest, never afraid to bare her soul to Shea even when Shea didn't deserve it.

If Shea wanted Ruby, she would have to show Ruby all of herself. It was only right.

So Shea started, voice wavering and meek

in the night: "We were assigned to an eyewitness. A man who was in debt with the wrong sort of group. When he didn't pay up, they went after his family; killed his wife. He agreed to testify in court, and we took it from there."

Ruby said nothing. Only waited. Shea couldn't look at her anymore, so she played with a loose thread dangling from her pillowcase, the warmth at her back a comfort rather than a burden.

"I don't know how they found the safe house. We never found out. But they did, and we were ambushed in the middle of a night shift. I tried to get the witness out of the house while the other officers handled the group, but one of them was waiting for us around the back. I was stupid enough to try to act brave, so I fought back and told the witness to run. And then when I realised he had a gun, I had to stop. I tried to get to the witness then, but Kate...." Shea choked on the words, on the memory. She could still taste gravel in her mouth, still hear Kate's shouts: *Get the witness, Shea! Protect the fucking witness!* But Shea hadn't followed the rules. She hadn't done her job that night. "My partner, Kate, came out of nowhere from the other side of the house, and he pointed the gun at her instead. I had to choose and... I made the wrong choice. I failed. I went for Kate. I had to choose Kate. I threw myself on top of her at the same time the suspect fired, and I was shot instead of her."

Tears brimmed in Shea's eyes, but she blinked them away, unwilling to let them fall. Not now. Not when she had come so far from that night.

"Jesus, Shea." Ruby sounded as though the wind and the words had been knocked out of her. As she shifted, her dark hair fell across her face like a curtain, until Shea had to search to find the concern written across her features. "What happened? To the witness? To Kate? To you?"

"The witness was killed. After the suspect shot me, he shot the witness too." The words were hollowed out by three years' worth of grief. Of regret. Of replaying that night in bed every night and hoping for a different outcome. "It was my fault."

"No—"

"It was," Shea said firmly. "It was my fault, Ruby. My job was to protect him, but I protected Kate instead." Because she had seen that gun pointed at her partner and lost her mind. Because Kate hadn't just been her partner, but something else, something forbidden and unprofessional — for Shea, at least. The feelings hadn't been reciprocated. "Kate and the other officers managed to catch a few of them. They're all locked up now. I… I was off my feet for a long time. Lost a lot of mobility in my legs."

Paralysed. Numb. That was what she had been. And all the feeling absent from her legs had burned a hole of anger in her heart instead. She had to figure out who she was when she couldn't walk, couldn't move properly, couldn't get out of bed and put on her work uniform.

"So you *had* to retire," Ruby concluded. "How long did it take to recover?"

"Well over a year. I was in a chair for a while, did a lot of physical therapy and rehab. But that's not really why I had to retire. I had to retire because a man died under my watch, Ruby. Because I let him."

And tomorrow, Shea would have to face it all again.

"You were looking out for your partner." Ruby's hands pulled away from the scars to brush through Shea's hair, thighs pressing against thighs, hips pressing against hips — soft against sharp. "You had to make an impossible choice, Shea. There aren't many people who would take three bullets for *anyone*."

Shea sucked in a sharp breath, her jaw clenching as she twisted to look Ruby in the eye. "I wouldn't make the same mistake twice. I wouldn't let somebody I'm supposed to protect get hurt again. Ever. You know that, don't you?"

A light, disbelieving shake of Ruby's head. "You're *not* supposed to protect me. It was never *your* job."

"But I chose to, and I'll keep at it until I get you out of this." Shea placed her hands beneath Ruby's chin, the pad of her thumb resting just below the curve of Ruby's bottom lip. "I mean it, Ruby. I will."

"I know." There was no doubt in Ruby's gaze, no fear. Even after what Shea told her, Ruby trusted her completely. Shea would make sure it stayed that way. "Just don't jump in front of any more bullets." Ruby's hands fell back to the scars… and then daringly lower. "I want us both to get out of this. Together."

Shea couldn't make any promises. She would sooner risk herself again than let the bastards trying to kill Ruby have their way. Still, she nodded and let Ruby kiss her, let herself get lost as Ruby's hands slid past Shea's tailbone and into the waistband of her pants. And she found herself wondering why she had spent so long hiding away.

Tonight, Ruby had seen all of her and she didn't run, or judge, or hate Shea for it. She understood. She shared the burden. Two shattered souls welded together — stronger as one.

So Shea kept Ruby as close as she could, keeping them both strong until dawn slipped in like an intruder through the windows and tomorrow became today.

CHAPTER ELEVEN

Ruby's first mistake the next day was turning on the small television in the corner of the bedroom while Shea showered. They'd had breakfast downstairs with conversations led by Bridget that nobody should have to endure before nine a.m., but Ruby's nervous stomach was at least filled with scrambled eggs and hash browns now. Flint sat beside her as she flicked through the channels: weather forecast, *Everybody Loves Raymond*, teleshopping, the news, *Fireman Sam*—

She only registered what she saw once the breaking news headlines merged into the animated children's show. Her face on the news. Her name. Heart somersaulting into her throat, Ruby went back to the previous channel and immediately wished she hadn't.

Gen Y's lead singer, Ruby Bright, pronounced dead after fatal car accident in Cumbria.

She couldn't hear what the reporter was saying through the thunder in her ears. Something about the band, about how it had only been six weeks since Ezra was killed the same way. How it was a huge loss to the music industry.

Ruby felt like screaming, but the reporter's next words stopped her: "Ruby's family were said to have been informed of the news this morning and have since put out a statement claiming that they wish for time and space to process their loss. Maxine Oliver, Gen Y's only remaining band member, posted a powerful image on Instagram just an hour ago of the band at a show in Prague earlier this year, the caption left blank. We can only imagine what sort of grief the twenty-five-year-old bassist must be going through at such an awful time, less than two months after surviving a tour bus crash that resulted in both guitarist and vocalist Ezra Lawson's and drummer Spencer Wood's death."

Her family. The image cut to another report, a lottery winner who had spent all his winnings on a waxwork of himself only to have it melt after being left beneath an air vent, but Ruby was frozen on the mention of family.

Her aunt thought she was dead. Everybody thought she was dead. She couldn't put her family through that, not after the death of her parents, not after everything. And then the footage cut back to Ruby's story, displaying a tear-stricken, pale-faced Cerys.

It was a pre-recording of a press conference addressing Ruby's death. Cerys kept pausing between words like "tragedy" and "loss" to choke back a sob. Next to her, Mason sat and nodded with his hands clasped together on the desk.

Anybody watching would think that hunched posture and lowered gaze a sign of sadness, but Ruby had seen Mason's reactions to cancelled gigs and missing artists and plummeting sales, and she'd also seen him trying to hold back his excitement in meetings: that cool, calm collectedness that concealed the greed and disregard for his client's well being, and that's what this was. Later it would change to appear solemnly respectful, when they announced that *Gen Y: Greatest Hits* would be released later today, along with demos that had never seen the light of day before now.

One of them played as a world exclusive after the press conference faded to black. A song Ruby had written for the first album. It had been rejected immediately: too solemn, too depressing, too whiny. Had they just been saving it for now? To play her as the tragic heroine in Fusion's story?

God, she wasn't even dead yet, and they were already profiting off it. This had been their plan all along: to shut her and Ezra up before they could expose Fusion as the monsters they were and then let the money roll in afterwards.

It made her feel sick. She hunched over herself, waiting to taste the acid, waiting to rid herself of the greasy breakfast Bridget had made for them, but nothing came.

And then anger did. Anger, and the need to know the truth about her manager. How long had Cerys known? How could she sit there and pretend to cry over Ruby's death after everything they'd been through? They were *friends*. Cerys had been sympathetic about it all. She even held Ruby's hand in the hospital after the crash.

Ruby snatched up the telephone from the bedside table and dialled her number before she could think better of it. She couldn't stay silent anymore. Not now. The phone only rang twice before a breezy — though slightly hoarse — voice sounded from the other end. "Cerys Watson of Fusion Management," was her familiar greeting.

"Cerys." Ruby gritted her teeth, gripping the phone with so much force that it felt as though her knuckles might split open her skin.

A pause, one that was filled only with the sound of the shower in the bathroom, the steam curling beneath the door. And then, in a whisper so weak Ruby almost didn't hear it: "Oh, God. Ruby?"

"Did you know?" Ruby asked, voice cracking.

"You shouldn't be calling me." Cerys's voice remained low, taut.

"Answer the question!" Ruby wasn't just angry for herself. She was angry for Ezra. Cerys had taken care of him too. She had been his friend too. Had she known he was going to die? Had she sat, holding Ruby's hand, comforting her, *knowing*?

"I didn't know. I swear I didn't. Not until yesterday. I'm trying to get out, Ruby, and you should too. You need to run. Stay hidden. If they find you...." The sentence remained unfinished, broken off by an anxious sob and a curse. "I knew they were bad, Rubes, but I didn't know it would come to *this*."

"What did they tell you?"

"They told me that if you contacted me, I was to tell them. I won't. Of course I won't. I just need to find a way to get out. The whole fucking office is like something from bloody James Bond. They've hired all this new security, and they're always bloody watching us."

Ruby didn't know if she believed her. At the end of the day, Cerys enjoyed the hefty salary she earned at Fusion as much as Mason did. She would probably do anything to keep her job. And if she was being watched, there was nothing to stop her from telling Mason as soon as she hung up the phone.

Even so, Ruby wanted to believe that their friendship had at least been a little bit real. That Cerys — warm, bubbly, charming Cerys — couldn't be as cold and murderous as her employers. "If anything about our friendship was real, Cerys, I need you to do something for me."

"Yes," Cerys breathed. "Anything."

"Tell my aunt I'm not dead. Tell her the truth. Find a way to get her safe. Please—"

"What on earth are you doing?" Shea's sudden bark left Ruby's plea suspended across the line. The phone was snatched from her and smashed back onto the receiver, Shea's features, damp and shower-streaked, blazing with fury. "I told you not to call anyone!"

Ruby didn't know how to respond at first. She had never been confronted by an angry woman wrapped in a towel after just finding out that the entire world thought she was dead. She could only point to the TV still blaring, now with an image of the SUV being fished out of the lake in Cumbria. "They told everyone I was killed in the crash."

"*What*?" Shea whipped around and almost lost her towel in the process. Ruby watched the anger step aside to make room for understanding, sympathy — and then white-hot fury. "Those *bastards*!"

"I had to know," Ruby whispered. "I had to know if my manager was in on it. I had to tell someone to make sure my aunt knew the truth."

"Ruby…." Shea swallowed a jagged breath, at a loss for the first time since Ruby had known her.

"How are we going to find a way out of this?" It was the doubt that broke Ruby in the end; the doubt that made her want to crumble into ash and have her remains swept under the carpet. Half of the world thought she was dead. The other half *wanted* her dead.

"We just will." Shea's voice hardened, and she risked removing a hand from the top of her towel around her chest to cup Ruby's cheek. Her green eyes turned to precious, unshatterable stone.

"How?"

Shea didn't even let her finish the thought. "Because I refuse to let them win. It ends today, Ruby. *We* end it today, you and me. For everything they've done to you. For the people you've lost."

It was all Ruby needed. Shea was right. Fusion couldn't win. Not after Ezra. Not after Liam. Not after this. Ruby would make sure they paid for all of the pain they'd caused. She would get her best friend his justice. She would fight to her last breath and, with Shea by her side, she wouldn't face it alone. Ruby wanted to be as strong as Shea, and she would be.

Ruby nodded, defiance flaming in her bruised and broken features. "It ends today," she agreed.

❊ ❊ ❊

Ruby's hand hadn't left Shea's since boarding the final train to London Euston. Shea couldn't pretend she wasn't glad for it. At least this way, she could feel Ruby's warmth, know that she was beside her and safe.

They had left Flint with a more than willing Bridget, and Shea suspected that if — *when* — they returned to The Elm Tree Inn to collect him, he might have acquired a few knitted tea cosies and bow ties and an extra stomach from all of the sausages Bridget liked to feed him.

Ruby remained quiet as green landscapes

slowly merged into the grey stone and towering office blocks of London. Shea squeezed her hand, knowing better than to ask if she was okay. "It's nearly over," she whispered instead.

Over the tannoy, the final stop was announced by an obnoxiously chirpy conductor. Shea stood and Ruby followed as she made her way to the end of the carriage, the engine humming beneath her feet. As the platforms came into view, she narrowed her eyes and reminded herself of the harsh, cool metal jutting out of her waistband beneath her jumper. She wasn't a fool. She knew that if the people after Ruby were going to wait anywhere, it would be in city train stations, especially ones so close to Fusion's headquarters. Shea hadn't fired a gun before, but there was a first time for everything. She would if she had to.

Still, when Shea caught sight of a man in a charcoal suit much like the ones Claire, Eric, and Leona had worn at the farm, panic charged through her veins. He loitered on the platform opposite, a phone to his ear as he checked his watch.

"Shea." Anxiety quivered in Ruby's voice.

"Stay behind me," Shea instructed calmly. "Keep your head down. If I tell you to run, do it. They can't hurt you here, not when everyone already thinks you're dead. It'd risk people finding out."

As the train sighed to a stop on the edge of the platform, Ruby nodded and huddled as close to Shea as she could, bowing her head so the visor of her cap bathed her face in shadows.

The seconds spent waiting for the doors to open felt like hours. Finally, they opened and Shea pulled Ruby onto the platform, heading straight to the set of steps leading into the centre of the station. It had been a long time since Shea had been to London, and she didn't have time to find the signs pointing to the tube station. She could only keep moving, keep hoping, keep feeling Ruby's presence brushing against her back, her arm. They would get out of here. There was no other option.

Skipping up the steps two at a time, they followed the current to the ticket barriers. Shea couldn't afford to look behind her to see if they were being followed, though her back prickled with apprehension. It didn't help when they spilt out into the main station hall and everything assaulted her at once: the mingling odours of greasy fast-food restaurants and buttery pastry shops, the overwhelming din of conversation and the heavy bodies pushing to buy tickets and head into stores. Too many signs with arrows pointing in different directions, too many notice boards and people and—

"This way." Ruby tugged Shea through it all, down a set of stairs. The air turned colder as they made their way underground, all daylight and colour leached by the unpolished silver escalators and fluorescent lights. Everything echoed eerily down here, the trains coming and going with huffs that whispered through the graffitied tunnels.

They'd nearly made it.

"Which station do we need?" Ruby asked.

"Westminster." The words on the departure boards blurred, and it was Ruby who knew where to go, what to do. They came out onto the platform, breathless and desperate for a train to roll in. Shea could feel it all closing in on her: the suffocating tunnels and the noise and the earth closing in on them from above and… *them*.

Two officers: the man who had been on the platform and a woman who must have joined him on their way down. They found them.

Shea ushered Ruby further down the platform to the ticket machines, but it was too late. The dark-haired man had already fixed a pair of narrowed, inky eyes on Shea and began shoving through the waiting crowds to get to them. Shea ushered Ruby to get behind her, reaching for the gun and curling her fingers around the hilt.

"Be careful," she warned when there were no more bodies or space between them. "You don't want to cause a scene."

The woman lingered at the man's side, both of them unblinking and tall and square-shouldered. They reminded Shea of automatons: postures stiff and not a hair out of place.

"I agree," the man growled, his long face reminding Shea of a Doberman whose hackles had risen defensively. "Hand her over and we won't have to."

"That's not going to happen." Shea's upper

lip curled in disgust as she glowered at both of them in turn. And then, when the man stepped closer, Shea drew out the gun and thrust it into his stomach as subtly as she could. "It would take less than a second for someone to recognise Ruby Bright. And then what? The world finds out she isn't dead, someone gets their phone out and records a video of you threatening her. You'd expose everything that Fusion has been trying to hide."

"I'm sure we can find a way to make this look like a terrible accident. It's nothing we haven't done before."

As though taking her cue, the woman slipped past Shea to grab Ruby, the end of a gun barrel jutting subtly from her blazer and into Ruby's ribs.

Shea snarled and dug her own gun further into the man's hard stomach, finger twitching over the trigger. "Please don't make me shoot you here. It would be an awful job for the cleaners to deal with later."

His dark eyes twinkled as though he found it all an amusing game. Shea couldn't help but flinch when he lifted his hands and curled them around the nose of her gun. "We were warned about you, Shea O'Connor. Obedient little guard dog. You're supposed to be retired. Of no use to the force anymore, anyway. I can't say I'm all that intimidated by you.

"You're outnumbered, Miss O'Connor. Know when to give up."

Rage swelled in Shea like a tidal wave, ready to obliterate anything in its path. And *they* were in her path. They were threatening Ruby, the woman Shea….

She couldn't finish that sentence yet. Not until they were out of this safely. She could let it all descend into chaos now, pull the trigger, but a gun was pointed at Ruby and she couldn't risk it. Instead, she nodded and let her shoulders sag in resignation.

"At least you're smart." The corner of the man's mouth curled with an arrogant smile. Shea wanted to slap it off his face. Instead, she took a step back so that she was beside Ruby. Shea couldn't look at her, couldn't let her see the fear. This might not work. This probably wouldn't work.

She placed her gun back in her waistband and tilted her chin to signal surrender. The woman did the same a moment later, though her hands remained clutched around Ruby's upper arm, biting into her jacket.

The man smirked crookedly and shoved his hands into the pockets of his tailored trousers. *Arrogant prick.* "Let's go."

His words were drowned out by the sudden rattle of an oncoming train, the one that would take Shea and Ruby where they needed to go. Ruby glanced behind her as they began to lead her away, her eyes round with pleas, with terror. Swallowing, Shea waited just a moment longer, listening for the train to get closer, closer, closer. The lights flickered around the tunnel's corner, illuminating a shaft of sooty stone.

Now.

It took three steps to get behind them again. Their arrogance had made them ignorant, unsuspecting. They had underestimated Shea's commitment to the cause. A mistake.

Shea used their turned backs to her advantage, pulling her gun out and pointing it at the woman's head at the same time she thrust her boot into the back of the man's knees. He fell to the floor, and Shea didn't waste a moment in pulling Ruby behind her again at the same time the train shuddered into the station. The gun remained still in Shea's hand as she kept it locked on the woman's head, the man rolling over and pulling himself up to his elbows with bitterness twisting across his cruel face.

"Get on the train, Ruby." It came out not as an order but a warning. Things were about to plunge into chaos. It was confirmed when a few passengers waiting on the platform noticed the gun and gasped. Most of them scuttled either onto the train or back up into the station.

"Shea—" Ruby began to argue, but Shea didn't have the time.

She pressed her boot onto the floored man's chest to keep him down. *"Get on the train!"*

Ruby's lips parted, but she was clever enough to swallow her words this time, hopping on the train through the nearest door. Shea could feel her eyes on her from the window — and a dozen others with them.

The woman pulled out her gun again at the same time the man kicked Shea's from her hands. She was thrown to the floor roughly, gun clattering across the platform, out of reach. But she wouldn't go without a fight, so when cold metal bit into the nape of her neck, she turned and swiped it away to deliver another boot to the woman's stomach. It sent her stumbling backwards, giving Shea time to stand.

The man was rising to his feet again too, and she knew she couldn't fight both of them at once, not when the woman was aiming the gun at her again. With a grunt, she pummelled into the man and punched the smirk from his face just like she'd wanted. If she kept moving, the woman wouldn't be able to aim.

Her knuckles split as she hit him again and again, her legs straddling him and blood filling his mouth as he bellowed, "*Shoot* her!"

Shea didn't give her a chance. They writhed, elbows jabbing ribs until Shea broke free. The train door was inches away, and she only had moments to get on it before it left the station. Shea caught sight of Ruby peering at her from the window, face twisted with heart-wrenching worry, and she knew what she had to do. She knew where she was needed.

The woman must have known, too, because

as Shea sprinted onto the train, sharp, stinging pain scored across the side of her arm. Shea bit down on her tongue so hard she tasted the metallic tang of blood. As she collapsed into the carriage, the doors drew shut like heavy red theatre curtains.

She could only sob with half-agony, half-relief when the train heaved forward and her attackers slid away into shadows. Above her, the lights blinked, and she glanced up at them to distract herself from the gaping wound beginning to ooze crimson.

"*Shea!*" Ruby's voice rent through the adrenaline rush, and then she was in front of Shea, her brown eyes glossy and her hands clutching onto Shea for dear life. "Shit. Shit, you're bleeding!"

Looking at Ruby's hands covered in her sticky blood made Shea dizzy, but she sucked in any strength she could find and used it to sit up and pull off her jacket to inspect the damage. "I hope Bridget doesn't want her clothes back after this."

A choked scoff exploded from Ruby's throat as she turned up Shea's wool sleeve. Through all of the blood, it was difficult to make out how bad the wound was.

Shea's eyes fell past Ruby then, realising that she had an audience. None of them offered help, probably none too keen after what they had seen her do on the platform. Shea forced a strained smile. "Are you all going to stand there and stare at me?"

"*Shea*." Ruby tutted and dabbed at Shea's wound with her coat. The other passengers only glanced at one another, bewildered, and then scattered. "What did I tell you about jumping in front of bullets?"

Flinching, Shea studied the gash on her arm. There was no sign that the bullet had torn through muscle. In fact, it had barely touched her, and the rivulets of blood were just the melodramatic result of a superficial wound. "It's just a graze. It must have skimmed me."

"Are you sure?" Ruby didn't look convinced. Her face remained sickly pale, thick brows drawn together. "Shouldn't I rip my shirt to use it as a tourniquet or something?"

Shea would have laughed if she wasn't in so much searing pain. "No use wasting a good shirt. She clearly wasn't a great shot. I'm fine, really."

"You're a fucking martyr is what you are. You could have been killed!"

"I got us out of there, didn't I?" Shea snapped back impatiently.

"Just about. You should have just let them take me!"

"*No*." The word dripped with venom at the thought. There had been just a whisper of a moment on the platform where Shea hadn't known if she *could* get Ruby safe again, and that fear was worse than any gunshot wound or beating. "I told you I'd get you out of this and I will."

"At what cost?"

"At *any* cost!" Shea hauled herself up from the floor, molars grinding together as she stood on unsteady feet. The rest of her was fine. Sore and unsure, but fine. She would make it to the police station, to Kate, and they would be safe and more or less in one piece. There were no other options.

Ruby hovered around her and it only annoyed Shea more. Now wasn't the time for Shea to be treated like a sick patient on her deathbed.

"That's not good enough for me." Ruby's throat bobbed as she swallowed and lowered her voice pointedly.

"Don't argue with a woman who's just been shot, Ruby. It won't end well." Shea clutched her elbow to keep her arm as still and undisturbed as possible. Maybe she did need that bloody tourniquet after all.

"*Shea.*" It was a whisper that left Ruby now: a plea. Shea's focus fell back to Ruby to find her eyes swimming with something that caused Shea more pain than her wound. "I've lost too many people because of them already."

Guilt and sympathy and aching uncoiled in Shea's gut. She thought of Liam, lifeless on the bank of the pond. The way Ruby spoke about and grieved for Ezra. The fact that the world thought Ruby was dead and how disconcerting that must feel. And Shea couldn't help but soften, staunching Ruby's tears with the delicate pad of her blood-stained, trembling thumb. Her knuckles were bloody and torn. "You're not going to lose me, love. The worst is over."

Shea didn't know if she believed it. But Ruby leaned closer as the tube stopped at the first station, pressing her feverishly hot forehead against Shea's and allowing the ghost of a smile to sit on her lips. "Now we both have a bad arm."

"We make a good pair." Shea couldn't help but snort at the fact, peppering a gentle set of kisses from the centre of Ruby's brows down to the upturned peak of her nose.

Ruby's cap had slipped off her head slightly. Shea pulled it back on as a horde of passengers piled onto the train and then rolled down her sleeve to hide her arm to avoid more attention. They ended up pressed together in the lunchtime rush, choked by the smell of body odour and a commuter munching on a tuna sandwich.

But they were on their way to safety, closer than they'd been since this started. Shea let that knowledge keep her confident, keep her together. She forced herself not to think about what seeing Kate would be like after all these years. Forced herself not to think about anything but the woman next to her, relying on her even if she said otherwise.

Because she was all that mattered to Shea now. And all Shea wanted to do was fix the mess they were tangled in — and take Ruby home.

CHAPTER TWELVE

Ruby had never been happier to see the New Scotland Yard sign revolving outside of the police station. Somehow, they had made it with only Shea's bloody arm and bruised face to show for it. It felt like a miracle, and relief fizzed through Ruby as Shea led her into the building. They got into an elevator that took them to the fifth floor, full of offices and police officers milling about in uniform. Ruby felt incongruous at the edge of it all, but nobody seemed to notice the war-torn visitors. Not until Shea's name was called.

"Shea?"

Shea let out a breath of relief as the woman approached. She was elegant, and slightly intimidating, in a fitted grey suit, her cropped brown hair styled into a flat, sharp bob. The complete opposite of what Ruby had expected, though she didn't know why. She supposed she had just imagined somebody more like Shea: understated and rough around the edges.

"Your arm!" The woman stopped in front

of them to inspect Shea's wound, her expression seeming to crumple more with disapproval than concern. "Somebody should look at that."

"It's a graze." Shea shrugged it off. She somehow seemed tenser now than she had on the train, with her jaw locking and her spine stiffening. "They found us in Euston Station. I don't know how."

"Whoever they hired, they're good." Only then did the woman's gaze flicker to Ruby. If she recognised her, she didn't show it but had the courtesy to offer out her hand. "Ruby Bright, I assume."

"That's right." Ruby shook her hand, feeling uncomfortably meek and overwhelmed now that she was here.

"I'm Kate Wilde. I'm an old friend of Shea's."

Kate.

The name triggered a shrill alarm in Ruby's head. Kate was the woman Shea had told her about last night. The partner she took a bullet for. But Shea hadn't told her the detective who'd offered to help them was the same person.

Ruby frowned, eyes flitting between them. The only hint Shea showed of her unease was a muscle ticking in her jaw; she didn't look at Ruby.

They weren't just old friends. The way Shea had talked about her... Ruby wasn't a fool. She knew there was something more to it than that.

She didn't know why the suspicion left jealousy clawing in her gut.

"Good to meet you." It was a lie.

"We'd be better having this conversation in my office, I think." Kate didn't wait for any agreement, instead leading them down one of the corridors and into a small room decorated with wilting potted plants. A woman well-accustomed to people following her orders.

A computer sat at a desk in the centre of the office, three chairs clustered around it. Kate took the one in front of the window, leaving Shea and Kate to sit opposite.

Kate rooted through the drawers first, pulling out a roll of gauze and throwing it towards Shea with little acknowledgement. Ruby arched an eyebrow. *This* is the woman Shea almost died for? She was even colder than Shea.

Kate braced her elbows against the desk, shoving piles of paperwork aside in the process. "Shea told me a little bit about your situation on the phone. It's definitely your management who's targeting you?"

Ruby nodded, hands fidgeting in her lap. "They hired their security team."

"Any reason why?" Kate asked casually, as though Fusion might have been doing it just to kill time on a Sunday afternoon.

"They treat their artists poorly. I almost collapsed on stage a few times from exhaustion, and they made us lie about our personal lives. Our guitarist, Ezra—"

"The one who died?"

Ruby winced. It never got any easier to hear it, especially not when the question was delivered so tactlessly. "Yes. He wasn't happy either, and he threatened to publicly expose them for it all. That's when the tour bus crash happened and all this began."

"Okay." Kate tapped the desk with the tip of her pen, her features unreadable.

Shea cleared her throat. "So what are the next steps? Shouldn't this be the part where you arrest them?"

"Well, we can't do that without ample evidence. I've been searching since your call for something concrete, but they're hiding everything well. They'll slip up somewhere along the line, I'm sure, but for now—"

"We can't just sit here and do nothing!" Frustration simmered in Shea's voice and her hands curled to fists on the desk. Ruby fought the urge to reach out. It felt wrong to show her affection here, in front of a woman Ruby couldn't gauge the character of or the connection she shared with Shea. "That's not why we came here."

"I know that and I'm not suggesting otherwise, Shea. But we need evidence to make an arrest and—"

"I can get the evidence," Ruby volunteered without hesitation. Determination caused her to straighten in her chair. She knew exactly how she could get evidence. She knew exactly how to end this. It had been playing on her mind for longer than it should have been, as though she knew it would come to this.

Shea turned to Ruby in confusion. Kate only leaned back in her chair and gestured for Ruby to go on.

"Mason Milne is behind all of this."

"The director of the company?" asked Kate.

Ruby confirmed with a nod. "He won't expect to see me now. He thinks he's done his job — that I'll be dead in a few hours. I won't be. I'm going to walk into his office and I'm going to look him in the eye and I'm going to force him to admit what he did to Ezra, to me, to the rest of the band, and his other clients."

A snort of disbelief fell from Shea. "Just like that? I don't think it'll be that easy, love. Doesn't the place have security?"

"And I'm a client there to see my manager," Ruby shrugged. "He might not know that I came to the police. To him, I'm probably some naive little girl on the run, rocking up at my management because it's the only place I know where to go. I'm walking straight into his trap."

"He'll kill you."

"If that was an option, he wouldn't have hired other people to do it for him. I know Mason, Shea. He's an arrogant, manipulative bastard. If we're going to do this, I want to be the one to end it."

"No." Shea shook her head stubbornly. "Not an option. We'll find another way."

"By waiting and hoping some magical bit of evidence might appear?"

"Ruby's right." The words took Ruby aback, especially coming from Kate's lips. She had been lost in concentration before, but now she straightened and met Shea's eyes. "We can send her in with a wire while we wait on standby outside. Mason isn't going to expect to see her, and the element of surprise might just mean he slips up."

"And what if he doesn't? What if someone shoots her dead the second she walks in?"

Ruby glared and crossed her arms over her chest. She hated being talked about as though she wasn't in the room. "I spoke to my manager, Cerys, this morning. She sounded as though she didn't want to be a part of this. Said she only found out the truth about Mason yesterday. I'd bet anything that she'll be willing to help. She could get me into the office. They wouldn't hurt me in front of an entire building of staff, and they don't usually have security manning the back exit."

"You're awfully confident for a woman whose life has been threatened three times now," Shea accused. "Your plan is based on the hope that everybody in the building would rather stop for a chat with you than kill you. I think it's safe to say from experience that that's not the case."

"We don't know that," Ruby countered. "Let me try, Shea. Please. I'm not going to sit here a moment longer and do nothing. My family thinks I'm *dead*! There are people after me everywhere I go.

They killed my best friend. I'm can't let them put me in a corner anymore. I *won't*."

"For Christ's sake," Shea hissed, throwing her arms up in exasperation. "And you're just going to send a civilian straight to the people who want to kill her, are you?" The question was clearly meant for Kate.

Kate pursed her lips, eyes still narrowed in thought. "We can send our own officers in with her. Mask them as members of Fusion's security team. You'll have to sign a few forms, of course, but it's as good a plan as any."

"Unbelievable."

"We're not going to get a confession any other way, Shea." Kate sighed. "We can do this safely. It's entirely possible that this is the most effective way to do this."

"I can do it." Ruby took Shea's hand, no longer caring what Kate would think. It was the first time Ruby had ever seen Shea tremble; the first time Shea had ever let that stone-cold resolve evaporate to make room for the true fear behind the mask. Ruby understood. She was scared too, and she had been terrified when Shea put herself in harm's way. But Ruby trusted Shea because there was no one she'd ever met who was stronger, who Ruby believed in more. She only wanted that same belief returned. Ruby only wanted to be brave enough to finish this the right way, the way that she and Ezra deserved. "I'm strong enough to do it, Shea."

"It's not your strength I'm worried about." Tears glimmered in Shea's eyes, only for Ruby. Ruby didn't know what to do with them. "I'm not going to talk you down, am I?"

"Nope."

"Impossible, stubborn woman."

"You're one to talk." Ruby scoffed. "I'm doing this, Shea."

Shea glowered at Ruby without any hint of anger. In fact, it was awe that burned in her green irises. And then she squeezed Ruby's hand and said, "Fine. But I'm coming with you."

Ruby expected nothing less.

❊ ❊ ❊

"You're different with her." They were the first words Kate said as she curled the bandage across Shea's arm, covering the bullet graze until she had time to get it tended to properly. Ruby had left the office to sign forms and have the wire fitted, and Shea had just about been able to let her go without panicking again or telling her she couldn't do this.

It wasn't Shea's choice, and she couldn't keep Ruby from getting the closure she needed. It would be months, years, an indefinite amount of time waiting for enough evidence to take down Fusion otherwise, and they couldn't afford that when there was a team of bloodthirsty assassins searching for Ruby high and low.

Still, Shea wished she could at least go in there with her. The two of them had gotten through everything thrown at them this far together, but Shea couldn't follow her this time. She would have to sit, rendered helpless if something happened while Ruby met with Mason.

She couldn't let herself think about that for too long.

Instead, she lifted her gaze to Kate, waiting to feel the thunder that had once clapped through her heart for the woman. But while her dark features were familiar and not something Shea could ever forget, they didn't dredge up the same feelings they used to. She'd been in love with Kate once; hadn't been able to stand the thought of being without her, even when she knew it was wrong and Kate would never feel the same. Now, Shea could look at Kate without breaking. Now, she only had to face the shame of a past she'd never been able to forgive herself for with the only person who had witnessed her failure that night.

It was still difficult, but it was manageable.

"Am I?" Shea asked finally, calmly, as though it was normal to have a conversation like this three years after everything fell apart.

Kate only nodded, features moulded into that neutral mask Shea had once hated. It had meant she could never know how Kate felt. If Shea was a closed-door, Kate was an impenetrable vault. "It can't be easy, letting her go in there alone."

"No. It's not."

After tying the gauze, Kate stepped back to survey her work. "But you are anyway."

Shea shrugged. "I don't *let* Ruby do anything. It wasn't my choice to make."

"See." Something glittered in Kate's eyes, just for a second. Something that looked a little bit like pride. "Different."

Shea knew what Kate meant by it. She used to argue to no end whenever they were placed in dangerous situations — not for herself, but for Kate. Shea would have been better off working alone than with someone she cared for, someone she wanted to keep safe. It was the reason she had gotten shot, the reason why she no longer worked in the service.

"I don't regret that night," she admitted truthfully. Perhaps she *had* been too afraid of losing people then, too overbearing and protective, but at least they had both been able to walk away from it — even if her client hadn't. "I think I do sometimes; I'll always have to live with the life that was lost, and it's not easy; all that guilt. But if I could redo it, I wouldn't change it. Personal feelings aside, you were my partner, and I was never going to let you risk getting killed if I could help it. That night was always going to end with death. I couldn't let it be yours."

Silence ticked between them like an unsteady pendulum of a broken clock: suspended, unsure. And then Kate shook her head, her lips thinning with a smile. "You and that heart of yours, O'Connor. It's always getting you into trouble, even now. The truth is, I never knew what to do with it — the way you felt for me. I don't think I deserved it. I hope she does. I hope she gives you what I was never brave enough to."

The words left Shea speechless. Kate had never said anything like that before. She had never said anything about that night other than how wrong Shea had been, how badly she had failed at her job. She thought Kate hated her.

She tried to form a reply, but only empty space parted on her lips. This was foreign territory for them both. Shea, no longer vehemently in love with Kate, was able to set herself free from old shackles. Kate, giving Shea a glimpse of something real and new. If they could have been this way three years ago, maybe that night would have ended differently.

"The way I treated you after the accident was wrong," Kate continued finally. "It took me years to realise it, but it was. I concentrate too much on my job. On right and wrong. But being a detective has made me realise there *is* no right and wrong. People don't always act how they're supposed to act, and that doesn't mean they're bad. You saved my life and I didn't even thank you for it."

"No thanks necessary." Shea shrugged and then winced against the twinge it left in her arm. With the adrenaline wearing off, it was tender and heavy. "But thank you for saying it."

Kate smiled softly, and Shea couldn't help but return it. It felt as though a weight had finally lifted from her heart, one that kept her pinned down for years — not just because Kate forgave her, but because Shea realised that she forgave *herself*. She had made a mistake. She had failed in her duty. That didn't make her a bad person. It didn't make her less worthy of love. Ruby proved that last night when Shea told her everything and Ruby had listened without judgement.

She could stop punishing herself now. She could move on from her past. She could find closure. She just had to get through today first.

Ruby slipped back into the office from the corridor, her face pale and body jittery and restless. "I'm ready." It wasn't directed at Kate but at Shea.

"Are you sure?" Shea replied, and wished more than anything that it would be enough to make Ruby change her mind.

But Ruby and Shea shared the same stubbornness, so it was no surprise when Ruby tilted her chin proudly and said, "I'm sure."

"Then I'll get my officers in place." Kate's shoulders remained squared as she left the office, leaving Shea and Ruby alone.

Shea didn't move from where she perched on the desk, only able to watch as Ruby tugged at the hem of her cardigan. It seemed odd to wear a cardigan for something like this. Especially the crocheted, rainbow-patterned one Bridget had given her.

"Don't look at me like that," Ruby murmured finally, shifting between the chairs to inch closer.

"Like what?" Shea asked innocently, though perhaps she *was* staring. Memorising. Drinking in this confident, brave version of Ruby, admiring her for how far she had come since the day they met. It had taken Shea years to even begin to face her demons. It only took Ruby days.

"Like it's the last time you're ever going to see me."

Shea rolled her eyes. "That's not how I'm looking at you."

"No?" Ruby reached her at last and leaned into Shea, pressing her legs between Shea's.

"No. I know I'm going to see you tonight when this is all over. And I know that we'll go back to Bridget's together, and she'll make her wife cook for us; and afterwards, we'll lie together while Flint takes up most of the bed." Shea didn't know if it was the truth. She could only hope it was. She had no idea where she and Ruby would be left when all of this was done. No idea where Ruby *wanted* to leave it.

A watery giggle fell from Ruby as she tucked a strand of hair behind Shea's ear. "I like that plan."

Their lips met without urgency, without desperation. Certainty made the kiss soft and slow and unhurried, though not without hunger. Shea pulled away first, heart thudding out a steady melody in time to Ruby's breaths. *Not a goodbye kiss,* she told herself. *Not the last one we'll have.*

"Come on." Ruby's hand slipped into Shea's to guide her out of the office. "Let's go get a confession from the bastard."

Shea didn't let go until they reached Fusion's headquarters and she had no other choice. And then she sat in the unmarked police car outside with Kate and she waited for Ruby to come back to her.

CHAPTER THIRTEEN

Cerys met Ruby around the back of Fusion's headquarters, her eyes bloodshot and her fingers trembling around her mobile phone. She gathered Ruby into a hug immediately, overwhelming Ruby's nostrils with the opulent scent of her Marc Jacobs perfume.

"Oh, God, Ruby," she whispered shakily. "I'm so, so sorry. You have no idea."

"Thank you for agreeing to this," Ruby said. She had called Cerys at the police station to ask for her help in getting into headquarters and Cerys, though terrified, had agreed. Ruby's manager had always seemed so tall and confident before. Now, she was almost childlike with fear, her buttons done up wrong on her shirt and her hair scraped back into a messy ponytail.

"Of course. It's the least I can do. If I'd have known—"

"I know." Ruby nodded, all too aware of the two police officers dressed in plain black suits to blend in with Fusion's security flanking her on either side. There wasn't time for apologies now, and Ruby could only hope Cerys was as genuine as she appeared — that their three years of working together day in, day out meant something. "Is Mason in his office?"

"Yes. He's in there."

She sucked in a deep breath, schooling her features to show more courage than she felt. "Take me to him."

Cerys nibbled on her bottom lip and set off to the back entrance. There were never guards stationed at this door, not unless an upscale client was leaving the premises. The only problem was the security cameras.

Cerys used the keycard hooked to the pink lanyard around her neck to let them in, and Ruby made sure to keep the visor of her cap over her face. It was strange being back here knowing it would be the last time. How many times had she wandered into this place with Ezra at her side, being ushered and heckled by people who enjoyed controlling them too much?

In the end, maybe it was never going to end any other way. They had been locked into the contracts, had been shackled and stripped of autonomy. Now, Ruby would break free for both of them.

When they flooded into the elevator, it seemed to take twice as long for it to take them to the seventh floor where Mason's office resided along with other important company executives.

"Do you think it will work?" Cerys asked.

Ruby couldn't answer. She could only hope and pray, thinking of the wire taped to her torso and how it fed every sound straight back to Shea and Kate who sat outside, waiting. It was the only piece of security she could cling onto other than the officers. Shea wouldn't let anything happen to her. Shea would tear the place apart if it came to it.

The elevator dinged as they arrived on the top floor, and there was no more time left for comfort or final thoughts. They were here. Just a few steps away was Mason's closed office door, embossed with his name in gold lettering. Hatred sizzled like acid in Ruby's throat at the sight.

She didn't knock as she usually would, instead turning the door handle and inviting herself in without asking whether Cerys would follow. She didn't. She stayed in the corridor outside with the officers. Good. Mason wouldn't confess to anything if they followed her in.

Mason Milne sat idly in his swivel chair, his legs propped on his desk as he spun the scroller on his computer mouse. Ruby almost scoffed. His hired assassins were out on the streets, searching for Ruby, while he relaxed in here without a care in the world.

Well, until he straightened and realised who had just stepped foot in his office. London's skyline pierced through the huge windows behind him, the sunset bleeding through the spokes of the Millenium Wheel and sinking into the Thames. It stained Mason's outline with a violent shade of red — or perhaps that was just the anger flushing through him.

Ruby forced a smile and collapsed into the seat across from him, crossing one leg over the other as though she was any other client here to talk business. "Hello, Mason."

The door swung shut behind them, leaving the room in stifling silence. Mason's throat pulsed as he righted his collar and tie, his grey eyes scouring over Ruby. "What a pleasant surprise, Ruby."

"I'm sure."

"I didn't realise you were back in London."

"Well, considering you were announcing my death on the news this morning, I imagine not." Ruby clasped her hands together, trying not to grind her teeth. Her skin crawled in Mason's presence, disgust rising with the bile in her throat. This was the man responsible for Ezra's death. The man who had gotten too cooky and told the world Ruby was dead before he had even managed to kill her. He wouldn't get another chance at it.

Mason's cold features spread into false politeness: a smarmy smile gracing his lips, half-buried by a smattering of salt and pepper stubble. "It'll be true soon enough. Only a fool would walk into this office, Ruby. I thought you were smarter than that."

"Your people were having a hard time finding me," shrugged Ruby. "I thought I'd make it a little bit easier for you."

He cleared his throat and stood then, turning his back to Ruby to gaze upon the city. She wondered when his security team would come. Maybe they already had and the police officers were keeping them at bay. Maybe Mason hadn't called them yet because he was still in the habit of underestimating her. "Very valiant. You have to know that I didn't want it to end up this way."

"No?"

"Of course not. You were my best clients."

"Then why?" Ruby asked, her heart thumping and clawing like two hands reaching to pull the truth from him. So close. She was so close.

But Mason didn't take the bait. "Why did you come here, Ruby? To beg?"

"I came here for the truth," she said steadily, ice seeping into her tone. It had been fire until now, but seeing him, being here, the ghost of Ezra everywhere... It had drawn away anything warm about Ruby. Left her frozen and numb and as raging as a blizzard. "I want to know why."

"You're a smart young woman. I'm sure you can work it out."

"I want to hear you say it. I want to know why our lives matter less to you than your money."

A small hiss sucked between his teeth as his fingers danced across the top of his chair. "I've invested everything into this company. I don't like it when it's threatened by clients who suddenly decide they want to start making demands and threaten me with blackmail."

"*Demands?*" Ruby repeated incredulously.

"We only wanted to be treated like *people*."

"You were treated like gods!" he erupted, a green vein worming beneath the coarse skin of his neck. "You had everything and it wasn't enough!"

Ruby stood up then, brimming with too much fury to remain seated. "You took everything from us! You made Ezra hide who he was. You let us push ourselves to exhaustion. As long as the fans were happy and you were getting your money, you didn't care. You made us into your robots, and you expected us to let you!"

Mason scoffed. "Listen to yourself. Millions of people can only dream of having the life you had. It was *you* who threw it away, not me."

"No. People don't dream of what you put us through. I lost every shred of myself in this industry because of you. It was torture. It was *agony*. You made us miserable, and then when we stood up to you, you hired people to *kill* us. That's not a dream, Mason. It's fucking tyranny. We would have left silently if you just let us out of the contract. Why did it have to come to this?"

"It was business."

"It's *murder*!" Ruby couldn't help it anymore. Her blood was boiling, blotches of red staining her vision, and she slammed her hand onto the desk to prove it. It was made worse when Mason barely flinched. He genuinely had no regard for anything Ruby said. He didn't care. He didn't care that he had taken everything from her: her best friend, her freedom, her music. "Being targeted by your security wasn't in any of the fucking contracts."

"I wouldn't expect you to understand, Ruby." Mason fiddled with his cufflinks, brow arching as though *she* was being unreasonable. "And despite what you think, I am sorry it came to this. But I have to protect the empire I've built. You and Ezra were not the only clients I have, and I intend to keep this business for a long time to come. I won't let *anybody* take it from me."

Ruby chewed on her cheek. She still hadn't gotten a real confession from him. No matter how nauseous and livid she was, she had to keep him talking. Had to get it out of him, plain and simple, so that not even a top lawyer could find a way to wriggle him out of it. "So what will you do now? How will you make it look like an accident this time?"

He considered this, fingers inching towards the telephone on his desk. "I'm sure I'll find a way. Don't worry. A hefty percentage of your future royalties and savings will go to your aunt. She'll live comfortably from your work."

"And what about you? How do you live with it?"

His features twitched just slightly, a crack in his façade. Ruby used it as an incentive to keep prodding.

"You have a son, don't you?" She remembered playing Lego with him in the office once or twice. A gummy six-year-old who thought his dad was a superhero because he was always being introduced to celebrities. "How do you look him in the eye knowing you're a murderer? Knowing that someone else's son is dead because of you?"

"I'm *not* a murderer!" Mason shot to his feet, voice deepening to a rough growl.

"You killed Ezra. You're going to kill me. It doesn't matter if you're not the one to pull the trigger, Mason. Our blood is on your hands."

He let out a long, ragged breath, brows drawing together as though in thought. He came around the desk and gestured to the chair. "Sit back down and be quiet, Ruby. Don't make it harder than it has to be."

"Tell me!" she screamed. In the same instant, Mason thrust into her, driving her back to pin her against the wall. His forearm buried itself into her neck, choking and heavy. Panic seized Ruby, but she didn't let it consume her, not when she was so close. Instead, she locked eyes with him, features twisted into a glower.

"I had him killed," he hissed, "but I'd be happy to kill *you* myself."

"You're too much of a coward for that," she croaked out.

The police officers barged into the office a second later. Her own, not Mason's security. It seemed he had waited to call for them, or maybe he hadn't expected a fight from her — and now it was too late. "Mason Milne, you're under arrest for the murder of Ezra Lawson and Spencer Wood and conspiracy to murder Ruby Bright."

Mason went slack with shock again against her, terror turning his eyes into two silver full moons, half cast in Ruby's shadow. It was all the opportunity Ruby needed. She thrust her knee up into Mason's groin with as much force as she could muster, leaving him hunched in a pathetic heap at her feet.

"Ezra deserved better," she spat. "We all did."

It was all that Ruby had left to say. Relief rushed through her and she stepped back, leaving the officers room to cuff him and rattle off Mason's rights.

It was done. She had the proof. The victory was still barely a flicker as she watched Mason get hauled out. Ezra was still gone. The war was over, but her best friend wasn't coming back.

Cerys stood in the hallway, eyes filled with tears. She gathered Ruby into a hug when Ruby stepped out of the office. Her dark hair tickled Ruby's nose, her body wracked with sobs. "I'm sorry."

Ruby let her eyes flutter shut for a moment, gripping onto Cerys tighter though she wasn't really the woman Ruby wanted comfort from. "I know."

"They found some of the officers Mason hired downstairs. It's over, Ruby."

It didn't *feel* over. The world still thought Ruby was dead and the only person she truly cared about was downstairs.

Pulling out of Cerys's embrace, she took the

fire exit stairs on legs that didn't feel like hers, the spiralling of seven floors sending her dizzy. When she fell out into the fresh air, she could breathe again.

Not for long. Shea found her in less than a second and they collapsed into one another, Ruby's arms locking around her neck.

"Thank God!" Shea's breath filled the shell of Ruby's ear, and then she was pulling away, palms cupping Ruby's jaw to examine her face. "Are you okay? Did he hurt you?"

Ruby ignored the aching heaviness that remained pressed on her chest and shook her head. She hadn't even noticed she was crying until she tasted salt on her lips. "I'm okay."

"Good." Shea softened and pulled Ruby close again, planting a kiss on her forehead. "You did it, love. I'm so proud of you."

Ruby needed to feel these arms around her, holding her up, keeping her together before she could break. She needed to cling onto Shea until her heart stopped racing and she could breathe again. She didn't know yet when that would be.

Don't let go of me, she wanted to whisper but didn't have to — Shea wasn't going to let go. Not when they slowly made their way back to Kate's car with the sinking sun pouring onto their backs, or when they weaved back through the streets of London huddled together in the backseat, or when they debriefed Ruby on the next steps back at the station. Witness report. Trial. Press conference.

Kate offered to put them up in a hotel for the night, but Ruby could see the hesitation written on Shea's face. She wanted to get back to Flint. So did Ruby. The loving Labrador felt like home, an extension of Shea and now an extension of Ruby. She didn't want to be in London, lulled to sleep by sirens and drunkards and noise.

So Kate had one of her officers take them back to Alvechurch, and Ruby was glad for the fact that her cellphone had been confiscated weeks ago because she needed to shut the world out before it all became loud again tomorrow. After dinner — cheese and onion pies courtesy of Bridget's wife — she called her aunt, Shea holding her while she cried into the phone and told her story, Flint curled up on her knees. Tomorrow, the world would know Ruby Bright was alive and well, but tonight, she had one more night of just being Ruby, with Shea tied around her like a ribbon and exhaustion weighing on her like an extra blanket.

"You're safe," Shea whispered over and over as Ruby gradually fell into a deep sleep. "It's over."

And it was. For the first time since Ruby had started her career — it was over. They could finally rest.

EPILOGUE

In her brief break from fame, Ruby hadn't missed the blinding lights of cameras or the hundred different people calling her name as though they knew her, as though Ruby owed them something. She would rather be shovelling manure in the stables than face them now. But she walked onto the platform of the conference room with her head held high and Cerys's arm linked through hers, directed by Kate to sit in the centre of the long table.

She'd been given an extra two days. Somehow, they'd managed to keep the press at bay while Ruby was allowed to see her aunt in Peterborough. Shea had taken the opportunity to return to the farm — and had found out that Liam was recovering in hospital. They had revived him at the scene. By sheer luck, he was still here.

Shea stood at the edge of it all now, her blonde head just visible from where Ruby sat. Ruby hadn't asked her to come, didn't want her to sacrifice any more time from her life and responsibilities, but Shea was there without question. It was easier for Ruby, knowing she was there. They seemed to share the same strength, dig it up from the same hidden place within themselves — and it doubled when they were together.

Cerys began the press conference with an introduction. She explained the "mistakes" made by Fusion and how they had led to this, here. How Ruby's faked death had been part of the company's plot. She answered questions where needed, and then it was time for Ruby's statement.

All eyes and cameras fell to her.

Ruby sat forward and cleared her throat. When she spoke, the microphone echoed her words, making them sound wavering and haunted. Or maybe that was just her voice now. She didn't know. It had been a while since she last used a microphone.

"These past few months have been tumultuous, to say the least. Fusion Management had a duty of care to their clients, and in my case and the case of the rest of my bandmates, they didn't follow it. Even before recent incidents, I didn't feel safe or taken care of as an artist. My band and I worked twenty-three-hour days, and my health and wellbeing were put at risk on more than one occasion because of it. They also forced us to fake publicity stunts and imposed restrictions on our personal lives, deciding who we were allowed to be seen in public with and when."

Ruby took a deep breath, her eyelashes damp with tears. For Ezra. She would tell the truth that he couldn't; as much as was right for her to, anyway. There were things that weren't her place to talk about now, experiences that weren't hers to relay.

"As many of you know," she continued, "I had a very close relationship with my bandmate, Ezra Lawson. But while it was believed we were in a relationship, the truth is, we weren't. I loved Ezra dearly: he was my best friend and my soulmate. But that relationship was manipulated by Fusion's PR team to make it look like something more, and we were forced to go along with it even though it made us uncomfortable and meant that we had to lie on a number of occasions. And then...."

A pause. Ruby didn't know if she could do this.

Cerys placed her hand atop Ruby's and squeezed reassuringly, but Ruby's mouth was dry and her heart felt like it was trying to slip between her ribcage. It was instinct to glance back, to search for Shea, and she found her in clear view now, nodding and smiling supportively.

It gave Ruby the strength she needed.

"And then when Ezra decided to make a stand, to tell Fusion that their treatment of us was not acceptable, they targeted the band's tour bus in the hopes that an accident would silence us."

She looked up from the speech written in her hands, directly to the closest camera. "It didn't. While Ezra and Spencer were tragically taken from us along with many of the crew we worked with on tour, I survived Fusion's attempts against my life. I feel it's my duty to be transparent about the way the music industry and general public treat artists — this must change. Fusion tried to take everything from me, from withholding my rightful earnings in the first few years of my career to my best friend. I love music. I love performing. But it wasn't worth the pain that I and many others have had to endure. For that reason, I will be taking a hiatus indefinitely. It saddens me that my career has come to this conclusion, but it's necessary for my mental and physical wellbeing to take a step away and work through the pain that Fusion has caused me.

"I'm sure you all have many questions and, when the time is right, I'll try to answer them in more detail; but for now, I won't be taking further questions. After seven weeks of isolation, I'm ready to spend time with my family and loved ones. I thank you for your support."

She left it at that, rising from her seat with the static of the microphone shrieking in protest. Despite Ruby's request for no questions, the journalists began to hound her with them, and Cerys ushered her off the stage with the team of security before it got too rowdy. Ruby didn't take a moment to get her bearings before falling into Shea's open arms, a sob of relief pushed from her chest.

"It's done now, love," Shea murmured, her fingers lacing through Ruby's hair. "It's over."

Ruby nodded. She knew she had done everything she could. Mason was behind bars with the rest of his team. Fusion wouldn't come back from its crimes. Ezra had his justice, and Ruby had hers.

No more nights spent with ringing ears and an empty, restless heart. No more being told where to go and who to be. No more stifling her sobs in the shower of a hotel room in a city she didn't know the name of. She would be free again. And Shea would be here with her.

As she found her composure, Ruby drew away and pressed her forehead to Shea's. "Will you come visit me in Peterborough in a few days?"

"Only if you'll help me muck out the stables next week. It's a little bit harder with a gunshot wound." Shea had only needed stitches for her arm, and the thick wad of bandages was just visible beneath her sleeves.

Ruby snorted and echoed her words from the day they'd met. "I'm not a farmhand. You won't be using me as one now I'm your girlfriend."

She only realised her slip-up when Shea's brows rose high enough to touch her hairline. "Girlfriend? That's presumptuous of you."

Though heat flushed her cheeks, Ruby refused to take it back. "Girlfriend" sounded like a silly, childish label for somebody like Shea, and yet…. "Well, I know what I want."

"Good." Shea leaned closer again until Ruby could smell the toothpaste used that morning on her breath, the black English breakfast tea that had diluted it. "I do too."

Ruby would never get used to Shea's kisses, or the way her body reacted to them. The electricity; the knowing this was right, even when everything else was off-kilter. The farmhouse was never Ruby's safe haven: Shea was. And Ruby would carry it with her, along with the strength she never expected to have. It would be strange at first, navigating the roads between two separate worlds, but Ruby had the time and the freedom to do it now, and there was no one she'd rather do it with.

Ezra would have been happy for her. She smiled with that knowledge as she and Shea walked away from the platform and the journalists and the life that had torn Ruby down. She was ready to build herself back up and, despite everything, contagious, unmistakable hope drifted through her for the future. A future that was her own. A future with the impossible woman she was falling in love with.

The woman who would always keep Ruby safe and sound. Ruby had never doubted it.

ABOUT THE AUTHOR

Rachel Bowdler is a freelance writer, editor, and sometimes photographer from the UK. She spends most of her time away with the faeries. When she is not putting off writing by scrolling through Twitter and binge-watching sitcoms, you can find her walking her dog, painting, and passionately crying about her favorite fictional characters. You can find her on Twitter and Instagram @rach_bowdler.

BOOKS BY THIS AUTHOR

Paint Me Yours

Partners In Crime

Handmade With Love

Holding On To Bluebell Lodge

No Love Lost

Saving The Star

The Secret Weapon

Dance With Me

The Fate Of Us

The Flower Shop On Prinsengracht

Along For The Ride

The Divide